"Whoa, cowboy," she said. "How'd we get here?"

"I don't regret it," he said, looking right into her beautiful dark eyes.

"I have to," she said, standing up. "I'm not going there, Holt. I can't. If I help Robby this summer, you have to make me a promise that we'll be platonic. Don't flirt, don't sweet-talk me, don't come near me with those lips."

He stood, too. "Well, it's not going to be easy, but given how hectic my life is right now, I shouldn't be trying to start something with anyone." Especially not the one woman who could bring him to his knees. Sometimes he thought the real reason he'd left Amanda was because he knew she would have left him if she knew the truth about him, and he wouldn't have been able to survive that pain.

"So we have a deal?" she asked.

"A tough deal, but a deal."

"Shake on it. Cowboy's code means you can't break it."

He smiled and shook, mostly just to feel her hand against his, but inside he was sweating. Because he was already dreaming of breaking that code.

* * *

THE MONTANA MAVERICKS:
What Happened to Beatrix?

P9-CFO-563

Dear Reader,

When single dad and rancher Holt Dalton takes his young son to an animal sanctuary to adopt a dog, he ends up leaving with a bonded pair—a dog and a cat—*and* the surprise of running into his first love. Ten years ago, Holt broke Amanda Jenkins's heart, keeping his true identity a secret from her. Now he needs her help with his son and their new pets— and has to tell her the truth.

Amanda never got over Holt, and now the gorgeous, sexy rancher and his sweet son make it impossible for her to keep her distance—especially because she longs for a family of her own. When she and Holt strike a deal, suddenly, she's a big part of their lives and wondering if she can dare hope for a second chance...

I hope you enjoy Amanda and Holt's story. Feel free to write me with any comments or questions at MelissaSenate@yahoo.com and visit my website, melissasenate.com, for more info about me and my books. For lots of photos of my cat and dog, friend me over on Facebook.

Happy summer and happy reading!

Warmest regards,

Melissa Senate

The Cowboy's Comeback

MELISSA SENATE

HARLEQUIN
SPECIAL
EDITION

Special thanks and acknowledgment are given
to Melissa Senate for her contribution to the
Montana Mavericks: What Happened to Beatrix? miniseries.

HARLEQUIN®
SPECIAL EDITION™

Recycling programs
for this product may
not exist in your area.

ISBN-13: 978-1-335-89470-0

The Cowboy's Comeback

Copyright © 2020 by Harlequin Books S.A.

For questions and comments about the quality of this book,
please contact us at CustomerService@Harlequin.com.

Harlequin Enterprises ULC
22 Adelaide St. West, 40th Floor
Toronto, Ontario M5H 4E3, Canada
www.Harlequin.com

Printed in U.S.A.

Melissa Senate has written many novels for Harlequin and other publishers, including her debut, *See Jane Date*, which was made into a TV movie. She also wrote seven books for Harlequin's Special Edition line under the pen name Meg Maxwell. Her novels have been published in over twenty-five countries. Melissa lives on the coast of Maine with her teenage son; their rescue shepherd mix, Flash; and a lap cat named Cleo. For more information, please visit her website, melissasenate.com.

Books by Melissa Senate

Harlequin Special Edition

Dawson Family Ranch

For the Twins' Sake
Wyoming Special Delivery
A Family for a Week

The Wyoming Multiples

The Baby Switch!
Detective Barelli's Legendary Triplets
Wyoming Christmas Surprise
To Keep Her Baby
A Promise for the Twins
A Wyoming Christmas to Remember

Montana Mavericks: Six Brides for Six Brothers

Rust Creek Falls Cinderella

Montana Mavericks: The Lonelyhearts Ranch

The Maverick's Baby-in-Waiting

Visit the Author Profile page
at Harlequin.com for more titles.

For my aunt Arlene, with love.

Chapter One

Holt Dalton had turned around for three seconds—his attention snagged by two kittens playing with a piece of hay—when his son called out, "Look at me, Daddy!"

Holt's gaze shot up at the sound of the voice in the cat barn at Happy Hearts, an animal sanctuary where he'd come to adopt a *dog* for Robby. But they'd passed by the cat section of the "Adoptable Animals" barn first, and Robby had begged to go in after seeing kittens climbing up a hay bale.

Like kittens, like boy. Robby, seven-going-on-daredevil, was suddenly at the top of a huge stack

of hay bales, swinging back his arms as if prepared to jump—onto a shallow pile of hay a good
ten feet below. A few cats on varying levels of the
hay bales were watching him, while others were
either napping, doing a little grooming, or playing with toys and hay.

How his son had gotten up there so fast was
beyond Holt, but that was Robby for you. Look
away from the forty-eight-pound whirlwind at
your own peril.

"Robby, no!" Holt called up. "The hay won't
break your fall. You don't want broken bones
keeping you from doing all your favorite activities the last month of summer and playing with
your new dog."

"That orange cat jumped down and was totally okay!" Robby said, pointing at the tabby now
grooming himself in a patch of sunlight.

"You're not a cat, Robby," Holt reminded him.

And cats supposedly had nine lives. Robby
had *one* and was everything to Holt. He'd raised
his son single-handedly since his ex-wife had
left when Robby was three years old. Their marriage had always been rocky, but Holt had tried—
hard—and signing the divorce papers he'd been
served had felt like the ultimate failure. His ex
had made it clear before they were married that
she wasn't sure she wanted kids, but they'd gotten

pregnant accidentally. She now lived in Colorado with a guy named Enzo and sent birthday and Christmas cards with age-appropriate small gifts to Robby every year. Holt wished things could be different between his son and his mother, but Sally Anne had never deceived him about what she wanted.

"Cowabunga!" Robby shouted and leaped—without looking.

Luckily, Holt was right there with his arms extended and caught his boy, getting a kid-size foot in the gut for his trouble.

"Thanks for catching me, Daddy," Robby said with a huge smile, wrapping his skinny, freckled arms around Holt's neck for a hug. Not an impish, *ha-ha, you know I never listen* smile of victory. Just pure happy.

His dad caught him—and always would. Robby knew that. Holt's own father, Robby's gramps, would have said: *You shoulda let Robby fall, splat, right on the barn floor and broken a wrist or an ankle. That'll teach him. Being soft or coddled never got anyone anywhere.*

The problem was that his dad was right *and* wrong, just as Holt was both plenty of times. Sometimes you had to let a child learn a lesson. And sometimes *being there* was the right answer. Holt's life was a constant judging of that. Three-quarters of the time he thought he got it right. Like now.

He gave Robby's dark hair a tussle. "Robby, I said not to jump and that means don't jump. If I'd missed—"

"Like you'd ever!" Robby exclaimed, wriggling out of his arms and dashing to the glass door that led to the vestibule of the cat barn and exit.

"Robby, wait," Holt called, but his son was halfway up the path of the vast farm to where a bunch of cows were grazing in a pasture.

Holt was sure a few grays hairs had sprung out in his own dark hair. He headed after his son who was already chatting away with one of the cows, a Belted Galloway. Holt stood a few feet behind, ready to catch Robby if he ran off toward the barns again.

Of course he'd reprimand Robby for disobeying, for not following the rules about running around the animal sanctuary. But part of him always felt he needed to give his son some leeway, when it felt right, to be seven and do what was natural for him. Like running around a wide-open farm. Robby's first grade teacher had said he was a typical child, just rambunctious and that time and a little maturity would help. She'd given Holt some great tips that had worked wonders for her in the classroom—letting Robby take breaks and "shake out his legs," making sure he had a good snack, allowing him to use a squeeze ball that he could keep in his hand while she was instructing and listening wasn't easy. But the director of the camp Robby had attended a few days each week this summer had complained that the seven-year-old required too much of the counselors' attention and could he *please* speak to his son. That had made Holt feel like hell.

Even if he'd been expecting it. Holt had done his research on his son's impulsivity and consulted with Robby's teachers and the guidance counselor and read all sorts of articles. There was such a vast pool of information, with so many recommendations, that Holt would just do his best with what made sense to him. The guidance counselor had recommended getting Robby tested for ADHD, attention deficit hyperactivity disorder, at the start of second grade, to allow him to mature some, and that was what Holt would do.

He was about to call Robby over for a chat about following the rules—*and if you break another we'll leave*—but the boy was deep in conversation with the cow.

"I sure would love to take you home," Robby said to the cow. "I'd name you Daring Drake after my favorite Bronc rider. Or should I name you

Holt? That's my dad and he's my number one hero but it would be weird to name a pet cow after him, right? Anyway, Daring Drake is my number two hero. Want to know who number three is? You!"

As Robby continued to talk to the cow, telling the ole girl about the teacher he got for second grade, which started at the end of the month, Holt relaxed. Talking to animals really seemed to calm his son down. Robby wasn't jumping or running or trying to climb over the fence. He was just talking and fully engaged. Coming here, deciding to bring a pet into their home, had been a good idea. Holt had done his research, knew *he'd* be doing the brunt of the work, but Robby would have a living creature to care for and love, to talk to, to turn to.

"Is your dad your hero too?" Robby asked the cow. "Which one is your dad, anyway?" The boy glanced around the pasture, and Holt had to admit, his heart had moved in his chest. His son might be a handful, but he was incredibly loving. Holt considered himself very lucky.

"Awww," said a woman's voice. "That is sure sweet."

Holt turned around—and the man who thought nothing could ever shock him anymore felt his knees wobble.

Because there was no way Amanda Jenkins

was standing right there in the middle of Happy Hearts Animal Sanctuary in Bronco, Montana. He *had* to be seeing things.

But he blinked and there she definitely was.

Ten years older, yet it seemed as though she hadn't changed a bit. The same long, dark wavy hair halfway down her back. The same beautiful dark eyes and full pink-red lips. She was petite and had been on the shy side, not one to make herself stand out. But man, did she, then and now. The minute he'd laid eyes on her that long-ago summer they'd met while working at a camp for special needs kids, there were no other girls at Camp KidPower. Let alone Montana.

What could she be doing in Bronco, though? Neither of them was from here, though Bronco Heights was home to him now.

"Holt?" she said on a gasp, her expression as shocked as his must have been.

He nodded. "It's good to see you again, Amanda." Major understatement. He couldn't take his eyes off her as memories of their summer together hit him. All they'd shared and talked about. The feel of her lips on his. Her soft hands on his body. It might be August, but a chill, a good one, ran up his spine. Amanda Jenkins. The woman he'd let get away.

She didn't respond to that. "What in the world

are you doing in Bronco?" She glanced at Robby, still talking to the cow, then back at Holt. "And you have a kid. Wow."

He nodded and took off his Stetson, holding it against his stomach and running a quick hand through his hair. "I live here now. In Bronco Heights. My family bought a big ranch last year. Dalton's Grange. I have a cabin on the property for me and Robby."

He could see her taking that in—the *me and Robby*. Not *me and my wife and Robby*.

"You've been living in Bronco Heights for a year?" she asked. "I've been here two years. I can't believe I haven't run into you."

"Well, we never ran with the same crowd," he said. Also an understatement.

She narrowed her brown eyes at him. "The same crowd? We were practically the same *person*, Holt. Remember how we always used to say, 'I'm you and you're me'?" She smiled as if lost in the sweet memory, then frowned, then seemed embarrassed she'd said it. She lifted her chin. "Well, I don't know why I brought that up. Old stuff that doesn't matter anymore."

It did to him and always would. He remembered. The way they'd lie on the grass by the lake after they were free for the day—she'd been a counselor while he was on the kitchen staff—

holding hands, making out, talking about everything and anything. *I'm you and you're me*, she'd
say, and he'd repeat it back with absolute wonder in his heart, in his gut, in every cell in his
body. Those times when he was with Amanda
like that, just the two of them when it felt like
there was no one else in the world? Yeah, he was
her and she was him. But in reality? They were
nothing alike.

He'd never told her the truth—*why* he'd been
working at that camp, making industrial-size pots
of scrambled eggs and spaghetti and vats of "bug
juice" and scouring dishes and counters and mopping the huge kitchen floor. He hadn't told anyone. She'd made some assumptions about him
back then that he liked, that he was a college
student on summer break, as she'd been, and he
hadn't corrected her. For those nine, ten weeks,
he'd been the guy she thought he was. But that
was summer. Like all good things, it always came
to an end.

"Daddy, I definitely want a dog but I also want
a cow!" Robby called out as he turned and simul-
taneously rushed ahead, clearly having no idea
his dad was right behind him. He almost barreled
into Holt's waist and legs. "Oops!" He squinted
up at Holt in the sun. "See him, Daddy?" he said,

pointing at the Beltie. "His name will be Daring Drake after the greatest bronc rider in Montana."

"Hi there," Amanda said, extending her hand to Robby. "I'm Amanda Jenkins and you can call me Amanda."

Robby gave her hand a hearty pump. "I'm Robby. My principal at school always shakes my hand. I get called down to her office a lot and when I leave, she always shakes my hand. I like her. Some kids think she's mean but I don't. There was a girl named Amanda in my class last year. She was in the best reading group. I was in the worst."

Amanda seemed about to say something, but Robby beat her to it, his trademark.

"Can we adopt the cow, Daddy? He's the one I want." Robby turned and beamed at his new friend.

Happy Hearts Animal Sanctuary wasn't a working farm; it was a place where animals lived in peace and harmony with nature. The owner, an animal rights devotee named Daphne Taylor, rescued farm animals—and everything in between, from dogs to rabbits to guinea pigs—and gave them a home on the huge property. She adopted out the animals that would do well in forever homes, which was why he and Robby had come. To adopt a *dog*. Not a cat. Not a cow.

"That cow's a beaut—a female, by the way—but the cows at the Dalton Grange aren't pets, they're hardworking members of the ranch." His family ranch, where he, his parents and his four brothers lived and raised cattle. Daphne had full respect for the ranchers in the area, and he was glad to know that someone who had the means—Holt's father referred to her as "that hippie-socialite"—to run a sanctuary for animals had created this special place. Not all the ranchers in town understood Daphne, but Holt admired her.

"Oh yeah," Robby said with a frown. He turned to the cow. "Sorry, buddy. I can't adopt you. But maybe I could come see you sometimes."

"That would be very nice, Robby," Amanda said, her smile so warm that Holt wanted to reach out and squeeze her hand.

"Can you show us the dogs now, Amanda?" Robby asked, his blue eyes excited.

Holt glanced at Amanda. She wore a yellow knee-length dress with a short, fitted white blazer, and there were a few gold bangles on her wrist. Her shoes were flat but shiny and looked expensive. He doubted she worked here. Not in that dressy outfit.

"Well, I'm not involved with the adoptions," Amanda explained, "but I can find Daphne Taylor for you two. She owns Happy Hearts. I do social media for the sanctuary."

"Social what-ee-ah?" Robby asked, tilting his head.

"Social media refers to websites online—on computers—that let people communicate with one another in all kinds of ways. Facebook, Twitter, chat groups, that kind of thing. I promote Happy Hearts online and around the state so that people know about the animals and adoption events and fund-raising opportunities."

Robby nodded. "Isn't it so awesome that I'm getting a dog?" he asked. "My mom has a dog but I've never met him. Well, it's not really her dog. It's Enzo's. That's her boyfriend. They live in Colado."

"Colorado," Holt corrected, the neckline of his Henley shirt tightening on him. The way Robby talked about his mom just then, you'd think it didn't bother the boy at all that he'd barely had contact with her—and hadn't for four years. But it did. Sometimes, that stupid saying Holt couldn't stand—*it is what it is*—brought Holt to his knees, but it mostly just kept him from getting a decent night's sleep. Some things he didn't know how to fix.

Amanda's expression was a mixture of so

many emotions he couldn't pick out the strongest. Robby sure did like to talk.

"Well," Holt said, forcing a smile. "Let's go check out the dogs, Robby." Not that he wanted a fast getaway. Or any getaway from Amanda.

"I'll text Daphne to meet you two there," Amanda said, pulling out her phone and double-thumbing away. Seconds later she nodded. "Yup, Daphne will be over there in a few minutes. I'll show you the way," she added, tucking a swath of her long hair behind one ear. He noticed her delicate gold and ruby earrings, a sweet sixteen gift from her parents, he recalled. "The dogs have their own separated section of the barn with large cozy kennels that lead to outdoor runs for them."

She started walking and Holt had to tell his feet to move—that was how startled he was by her presence in the first place.

They went into the dog area, which managed to be sunny and shady, tranquil and energetic all at once. There were large white boards with dog names and schedules of who was walked when, and pegs that held many leashes and tables beneath with supplies, from dog food to treats. Robby walked up and down the rows of kennels, Holt trailing behind him, too aware of Amanda standing by the door and probably still reeling, as he was, from the craziness of running into each other ten years later.

Unless he was flattering himself. They hadn't exactly parted on good terms, and it was one summer out of her life. Maybe she hadn't given him a thought in all these years.

Robby was greeted by barks and dogs jumping up against the kennel doors. The seven-year-old stopped in front of the kennel of a medium-size black-and-white dog—a border collie mix, if Holt had that right.

Robby grinned at the dog, who sat staring at him, head tilted. He didn't jump or bark. The dog put his paw up on a bar of the door as if to say hi. Some dogs looked like they were smiling, and this was one of those.

"He likes me!" Robby exclaimed. "Hi. I'm Robby! I'm seven. I like running, talking, TV shows, Minecraft, cheeseburgers, ice cream, my grandparents and my uncles, and Daring Drake the bronc rider."

Holt glanced at Amanda, who was smiling. He had to admit, he liked that she seemed charmed by Robby instead of irritated by his happy chatter. He'd dated quite a few women the past couple of years, thinking about trying to settle down, to find his Ms. Right and Robby a wonderful mother. But any woman he'd been attracted to had not been mom material either because she showed no interest in Robby at all or because she couldn't handle his energy.

The dog wedged his snout through the bars as much as he could, his head tilted. One side was white, the other black, one ear white, one ear black, his furry body big sections of either color while his legs were mottled. The dog was particularly cute.

"Bentley is superfriendly," another voice said, and they all turned.

Daphne Taylor, around his age with long, wavy red hair and a warm expression, came toward them with a smile. Over a week ago, Holt had filled out an application to adopt a dog, then a few days later, Daphne had visited Dalton's Grange for a home check, scoping out his house and walking around the property. He, Robby and their cabin had passed with flying colors.

Daphne smiled at Robby and shook both their hands. "Nice to see you two again," she said. "I'll get a leash and let him out."

When Daphne brought the dog over to Robby, he fell to his knees in front of him and Bentley licked his face twice, calmly, not jumping, not barking, not knocking him over, then actually put his head on Robby's shoulder.

Holt almost gasped.

Amanda put her hand over her mouth.

Robby threw his arms around Bentley. "You really like me! I like you too." Bentley licked Robby's cheek again, his tail wagging. While petting him, Robby began telling Bentley his life story. "I was born in Whitehorn. That's a town in Montana. And then we moved to Bronco. You're gonna love Dalton's Grange. That's our ranch…"

Daphne's phone pinged and she excused herself for a moment.

Holt stood and read the information on the sheet attached to the Bentley's kennel. "Bentley, age four. Elderly owner surrender. Gets along with kids, other dogs, cats, animals, friendly and housebroken, nicely trained in the basics. Bonded pair with Oliver."

"Bonded pair?" Holt asked, looking at Amanda.

"Oh that's right," she said, biting her lip and clearly worried she should have said something earlier. "Bentley was surrendered with Oliver—a cat. They were raised together as a pup and kitten and they're very close. Daphne is firm on adopting them out only together."

Robby turned to Holt, his face falling. "Does that mean we can't get Bentley?" he asked, his lower lip trembling. He turned back to the dog and hugged him, the dog seeming to actually like the heavy affection. "Is Oliver your best friend? I don't have a best friend. You're lucky." He stood up and wiped under his eyes. "I think Oliver and Bentley should stay together. They're best friends."

"Well, I guess that means we're bringing them *both* home," Holt said, a sucker for bonded pairs. Plus he'd always liked cats. Sleek and independent creatures.

Robby's eyes widened like plates. He flung himself at Holt and wrapped his arms around his father's neck. "Thank you, Daddy."

"Now, the *three* of you will be best friends," Amanda said with that dazzling smile. "I'll text Daphne to bring Oliver on her way back in so that you can meet him."

Holt glanced at her. There was a time when he'd thought of Amanda as *his* best friend. Just for those two months that they'd been a couple, but she'd had a big influence on him afterward. He'd never stopped wanting to be the guy she'd thought he was. By the time he'd realized that, it was too late. He'd actually driven out to her college about six months after they broke up, but as he'd arrived in the parking lot of her dorm, he'd seen her going in with a guy, his arm around her shoulders Amanda laughing at something the guy had said. Holt had sat there in his car for a good ten minutes, feeling like absolute dog-doo, then had finally gone home and dated as many women as he could until he stopped thinking about Amanda Jenkins so much.

Robby beamed and wriggled down, continuing to tell Bentley all about Dalton's Grange, and that Oliver was going to love it too even though he hadn't even met Oliver, but if Bentley loved Oliver, then Robby would too.

Amanda was chuckling and wiping her eyes. "I'm sorry," she whispered. "But your son is adorable. I always think the animals that find good homes are lucky, but I know that Bentley and Oliver will be *very* loved and very well cared for."

Not that you took good care of me, of us, he imagined her adding. Which was nuts. Her expression hadn't changed. He supposed he just felt guilty at how he'd left things, even if she'd clearly moved on. She'd thought they'd figure it out once camp ended but he'd just walked away, barely saying goodbye.

This whole summer you made me forget that people can shock you, she'd called after him. *Maybe it's good you just reopened my eyes to reality.*

He'd stopped in his tracks and wanted to run back to her and apologize, tell her who he really was, no one that she'd want to be involved with if she knew the real him. A dropout. A troublemaker. He'd been arrested twice for stupid stuff, but he'd been in a jail cell, if only for less than an hour. His reason for working at Camp KidPower? Court-ordered community service. He'd been going nowhere fast at twenty-two, and Amanda had had the world at her feet. She hadn't had the easiest childhood but had been focused and self-motivated. Then again, her parents had been financially comfortable if on the negligent side, leaving her to fend for herself, which she had.

His parents had had nothing until his dad had struck it rich gambling just over a year ago, enabling his parents to start fresh in Bronco—specifically Bronco Heights, the "right" side of town for once. Holt and his four brothers would have stayed where they'd all been scattered across Montana, but their mom had had a heart attack last year, and the scare had made them all want to stay close, look out for her. His dad wasn't always easy to be around, even with money taking a huge stress load off his shoulders, but Holt had to say, he loved Dalton's Grange. And he loved having his family right there for Robby.

Daphne came back in with Oliver in a cat carrier and set it on the floor of the barn. "Oliver is four years old just like Bentley. He likes back scratches, playing with string and little balls, and curling up next to Bentley for his many naps. He's a real sweetie."

Robby knelt and peered in. "He's black-and-white just like Bentley! I love Oliver!" The boy stretched out on his belly, smiling at his new cat through the barred door of the carrier and now telling Oliver his life story.

"Looks like our little family just grew by two," Holt said, nodding at Daphne. "Let's bring our new family members home, Robby. You can show them your room. I'll bet that's where they'll want to sleep."

"Thanks to a generous donation from Bentley and Oliver's previous owner's family, Happy Hearts has everything you may need for them, from a dog bed to food they like, to brand-new bowls and toys," Daphne said. "I'll go grab those bags and the paperwork. We'll meet in the lobby in five minutes."

"I'm headed out," Amanda said to him. "I'll show you the way."

Headed out. No, he thought. Not yet. He could still barely believe he was actually standing a few feet from Amanda Jenkins. He was far from ready to say goodbye.

"Well, goodbye," Amanda said as she stopped near an archway—she certainly *was* ready.

"Thanks for helping me," Robby said, beaming at her.

She grinned at him. "My pleasure. Bentley and Oliver sure are lucky to be going home with such a wonderful boy who loves dogs and cats and cares so much about their friendship."

Robby beamed and looked at his dad to make sure he'd heard such praise. Holt sent her a smile of thanks. Amanda met his gaze and held it for a moment as if she wanted to say something. But she didn't.

Daphne came back in with papers in her hand. "Oh, Amanda—I just thought of something! Remember how we talked about you doing a story for the Happy Hearts website on a new adoption? How about you cover this adoption? Bentley and Oliver joining the Dalton family. It's such a great story—two best friends going home with a little boy to a beautiful ranch."

Holt raised an eyebrow. He noticed Amanda pale.

"Um, sure," Amanda said.

Holt nodded. "Happy to help."

"We're going to be famous!" Robby said to Bentley and Oliver.

Daphne smiled. "Amanda, I'll text you the contact info. And then you two can set a time for the interview. Get lots of great photos," she added.

Amanda managed a smile but looked like she wanted the ground to swallow her. "I sure will."

He was assured of seeing her again. Thank you, Daphne.

Even if Amanda Jenkins looked like she never wanted to lay eyes on him again.

Chapter Two

Amanda got into her car in the gravel parking area at Happy Hearts, expecting to hightail it out of there to put some space between her and Holt, but she needed a minute in her car to decompress. Maybe a few.

Holt Dalton. In the flesh. After all these years.

Her first love, her first *everything*. She'd had crushes and a few boyfriends before Holt, but when she met him at age twenty-one, the summer before her senior year in college, she finally knew what everyone was talking about when they used the words *in love* and *you'll know* and The One.

The tall, sexy, dark-haired, dark-eyed Holt, on whom every female KidPower staffer had had an immediate crush, had surprised her with his attention the first day. *There's just something about you*, he'd say, staring into her eyes, talking away, asking her questions, listening to her. He'd truly *seen* her, seen something exciting and irresistible in the shy, quiet, bookish young woman in the ponytail and glasses. She'd opened up with him, become more herself. She'd thought they'd always be together. But he'd just walked away from her at summer's end as if she'd meant nothing to him.

What did Amanda expect? she'd heard girls around her whisper on that last day, when everyone was hugging goodbye. *Holt the Hottie with Nose in a Book Amanda Who Doesn't Want People Calling Her Mandy? Like* that *would last*.

Well, they were right. And dammit, she didn't like people calling her Mandy because her grandpop had called her that her whole life, just him, and when she'd lost him, she didn't need people she barely knew giving her that special nickname because Amanda was too long or they wanted to tell her who she was. She'd tried explaining that to a blind date a few years ago, and he'd told her to lighten up. Sigh. Amanda was used to not easily connecting with people.

She slid down in her seat and glanced toward

the door of the barn where she could just make out Holt and Daphne sitting at a table, going over paperwork. No surprise that he had grown into a gorgeous man. Getting over him had been rough. She remembered how she'd forced herself to finally go on dates, mostly involving studying at the college library or the lounge of her dorm, and how she'd tried to *lighten up*. She'd had some short-term relationships over the years, no one measuring up to Holt Dalton. Until she'd met Tyler two years ago. She'd thought she'd finally met her guy and had gotten swept up in the whirlwind of them and had even agreed to his crazy, romantic plan of eloping to Las Vegas.

She turned to face away from the building, staring at the peaceful cows that Robby Dalton had been mesmerized by. She willed herself to think about the social media posts she'd schedule for Daphne and Happy Hearts and not let her mind go deeper into her almost-marriage, not right now, not after seeing Holt—talk about a double whammy—but the memories came.

Tyler had booked a honeymoon suite with the glittering lights of the strip outside their window, way up on the forty-second floor. That night, the plan was to go to the elegant wedding chapel in their hotel, her in the beautiful white dress she'd bought—not quite a wedding gown but still bridal—Tyler in his tux. Her handsome fiancé, a businessman she'd met through a work-related fund-raiser, had gone down to the casino to let her get dressed so he wouldn't see his bride until she was all dolled up. She'd texted him to let him know she was ready, but he didn't respond. Not to her texts or her calls. She'd waited and waited, pacing and calling and texting him, wondering what the holdup was, praying he hadn't gotten into an accident—she'd actually been about to call local hospitals—and then came the text.

I'm so sorry. The reality of almost doing this made me realize I can't. Sorry. You deserve better. I paid for the room till the morning, so no worries.

Right. No worries. She'd gotten herself together after ugly-crying for a good hour and checked out that same night, renting a car and driving north as long as she could before the tears made her eyes too blurry. She'd found the closest motel, somewhere in Utah, and checked in. In the morning she'd driven home to Whitehorn, Montana, and made some decisions. There hadn't been much for her in her hometown; her parents had retired to Arizona years before, she was so shy that she had few friends in town, and her job as the social media liaison for a county-wide bank was pretty dull. She'd typed *Best places to live in Montana* into her search engine, and the first town that popped up was Bronco, a bit farther north. It was part Wild West with an old ghost story legend, part glitzy with a vibrant but small downtown, and she liked that it was bigger and more diverse than she was used to. But best of all, a very good friend from college, Brittany Brandt, lived there, and she was looking for a roommate. Amanda had sent up a silent prayer of thanks to the universe for that.

Bronco, here we come, she'd said to her cat, Poindexter, and two weeks later they headed north. She'd instantly loved the swanky BH247 apartment complex with views of the mountains, indoor and outdoor pools, a hot tub and lots of singles. That was the strange thing about Amanda; she liked being around people and hoopla, just not for long. She'd pretty much stayed in her shell, much to her very outgoing roommate's chagrin. What would be the point of dating when it led to having your spirit crushed, your heart irrevocably broken, your trust obliterated? And so Amanda had focused on work, leveraging her social media and marketing work experience into her own small business, and now she had a solid list of clients, from Happy Hearts Animal Sanctuary to Bronco Bank and Trust. Since most of her work was online, intro-

verted, shy Amanda had found her sweet spot—
and on her sofa most of the time.

But then something happened that had changed
everything. Something very unexpected. Soon
after moving to Bronco, Amanda had walked into
Tender Years Daycare for a preliminary meeting with the owners on plans for marketing, and
those little kids singing their ABCs and running
around in the playground had stopped her in her
tracks. She wanted a family. A child. The feeling
had gripped her and hadn't let go. A baby. Problem was, she didn't want to have a child on her
own. Every time she envisioned holding a little
hand, there was a man beside her, holding the
other tiny hand.

A problem, since she wasn't letting a man anywhere near her heart, mind or soul for the fore-
seeable future. She'd thought Holt had broken
her heart ten years ago? Getting left at the altar
in her wedding gown had been a hundred times
more painful because it had taken her so long to
find Tyler, to let herself give into her feelings for
him, to open up. Then whammo, bye.

But if she'd thought ten years and a two-year-
old broken spirit would have protected her from
seeing Holt again, she was dead wrong. She'd
barely gotten through the twenty minutes she'd
spent in the Dalton boys' company.

That Holt was a dad wasn't a surprise. Back at camp, he hadn't been a counselor; he'd worked in the kitchen, but any time he had been around her campers, he'd been so warm and fun and kind to them. He hadn't ignored them or spoken down to them, hadn't been turned off by their special needs—and those issues had varied. He'd treated her campers like the individuals they were.

Maybe she'd tell Daphne she couldn't do the interview and photo session with Holt and his son—and come clean as to why. She and Daphne had become friends. Daphne, daughter of the richest family in town, had nonetheless been through her own share of life and would definitely understand. Amanda pulled out her phone but then put it back. Nope. She was a professional. Daphne was a great client, kept her very busy, and Amanda wasn't going to let her personal life get in the way. She'd just be all business when she went to Dalton's Grange, and that would be that. Holt had been in a town a year and she hadn't run into him, so after their interview and photo session, certainly another year could go by without her seeing him. Or his cute son. Or their precious new family members, Oliver and Bentley.

Feeling more in control of herself, she started her car, just in time to see Robby Dalton, his brown bangs blowing in the late-afternoon breeze, come out of the barn with Bentley on a navy leash, a matching collar around his neck. Amanda could see they'd already gotten Bentley his own name tag in the shape of a silver bone. Holt came out behind his son and called out to Robby to be mindful of the cars, but their truck was parked right by the barn. Amanda ducked down a bit, unable to drive away, unable to stop watching them. Holt was carrying the cat carrier in one hand, and two Happy Hearts reusable tote bags, filled to the brim, were dangling off his other wrist. Robby walked Bentley over to the grassy area in front of the truck as Holt put the carrier and bags on the floor of the back seat so that Oliver wouldn't be jostled, then Robby and Bentley got in.

When they drove away, Amanda realized she wanted to follow them, watch them introduce their new pets to their home. She shook her head at herself and turned on the radio to her favorite country station, as always playing a song about a love gone wrong. That would set her straight.

"Amanda, put on your dancing shoes!" Brittany called out as she came into the kitchen of the condo they shared. As always, Brittany Brandt looked fabulous in a strapless, billowy red jumpsuit and sky-high silver heels. Tall and willowy with light brown skin and long black curly hair, the thirty-three-year-old event planner—for Bronco Heights Elite Parties, no less—had just gotten home from work for a quick refresh of her makeup, change of outfit and a dab of her favorite perfume, which smelled heavenly. Brittany's social calendar was always packed, whereas Amanda's revolved around whatever binge-worthy TV shows she might watch. "DJ's is having a fundraiser and I've put you on the guest list," Brittany said. "Wear something swishy."

Amanda stopped midpour of the hot water from the kettle onto her herbal tea. She ran her free hand down her body, indicating her polka-dot yoga pants, long tank top, and socks with the cartoon owls. She did love DJ's Deluxe—the very popular upscale rib joint where their next-door neighbor, Mel, used to be the manager before taking a big role as CFO of DJ's, Incorporated—but after running into Holt she had zero appetite. "I've got a date with Poindexter tonight. There's a documentary on the history of Montana on that I've been meaning to catch. It even covers Bronco and the 'unexplained phenomenon' and ghost tours." Bronco had quite the history. No wonder it was always on "Best of the West" lists of places to visit and live.

Brittany raised an eyebrow. "Well, I'm not

gonna lie. That sounds good too. I wouldn't mind putting on my jammies and curling up on the sofa with a bowl of popcorn. But work calls! Sure you don't want to go? Lots of hot single men will be there." She grinned and flipped back her gorgeous wild long hair.

"I'm sure. Have fun, Brittany."

"I'll try to be quiet when I come in," her sweet roommate said, gave Poindexter a scratch on the back, then headed out.

Amanda looked at Poindexter. "Brittany and I sure are going to have different nights, Poin."

Her cat started grooming himself. Some conversationalist. Then again, if Amanda had wanted conversation, she'd be at DJ's with Brittany and a couple hundred of Bronco Heights residents. She hadn't shared too much of her romantic past with Brittany—Amanda just hated talking about it—but her roommate knew she'd been through the love wringer. The interesting thing about bubbly, constantly going-out Brittany was that she wasn't looking for a husband because she wasn't sure she wanted to have kids. The eldest of five siblings, her roommate liked single life and wasn't interested in a family of her own. *Yet*, Amanda figured. Men loved Brittany, and one day someone would likely turn her head even if Brittany wasn't too sure it was possible.

So Brittany liked dating but didn't want it to go anywhere because her biological clock was definitely *not* ticking, and Amanda's was ticking out of control but she hated dating because it either led nowhere or straight to heartache. No wonder they got along so well despite being very different. They were simpatico.

Amanda was about to turn on the *History of Montana* when her doorbell rang. She popped up and headed to the door. Her neighbor, Melanie Driscoll, dressed to kill like Brittany, stood there.

"Wow, you look amazing, Mel!" Amanda said, admiring her gorgeous hot pink dress—swishy indeed—and her sophisticated blond chignon. Mel's diamond engagement ring shone on her finger. Her friend had recently gotten engaged to Gabe Abernathy, from a prominent ranching family in Bronco Heights.

"I guess this—" she swept a hand down Amanda's outfit "—means you're not coming?" She grinned, knowing the answer would be no. Amanda stayed home unless she had to be somewhere for business reasons or to support a friend. And with the wealthiest ranchers in Bronco attending the fund-raiser tonight, her friends were all set.

"Poindexter and I are watching a documentary," she said. "It's been a long day. Trust me."

Mel's pretty blue eyes were sympathetic. "I get it. Listen, Amanda, I'm here because I'm ready to take you up on your offer to find out what you can about Josiah and Winona's long-lost baby."

Amanda squeezed Mel's hand. Not long ago, Mel had asked for Amanda's help with a very poignant family mystery, but then had asked her to hold off just in case Mel herself found any new information.

"I haven't been able to learn anything new," Mel said, "and all my searches have gotten me nowhere."

"Can you refresh my memory?" Amanda asked. "I just want to be sure I have it all straight in my head."

Mel nodded. "Beatrix Abernathy is the long-lost daughter of relatives of Gabe's. His great-grandfather, Josiah, kept a diary that was found buried under floorboards in the old Ambling A out in Rust Creek Falls, which his family abandoned before moving to Bronco decades ago. The new owners of that ranch were deeply touched by the seventy-plus-year-old old diary and its beautiful love story. Turns out, when Josiah Abernathy was a teenager, he had a secret love, a girl named Winona Cobbs, who'd always been on the 'delicate' side. Winona got pregnant, and I'm not sure of all the details, but she was institutionalized after she was told her baby died. But that was a lie."

"Oh my heart," Amanda said. "I wish you could say that true love won out, that mother, father and baby were reunited. I totally understand why trying to find Beatrix is so important to you and Gabe."

Mel's eyes clouded, and Amanda could see how affected her neighbor was by the story. "I keep thinking about poor Winona. How when she delivered, she was told her baby was stillborn and that Josiah learned that the baby was alive and well. How he wanted to raise her, but he was forced to place her for adoption. And remember, in a letter to Winona found tucked into the diary, Josiah wrote that he figured out who adopted his daughter and that someday, he'd bring her home. But I've done some digging, and no one has ever heard of a Beatrix Abernathy. So clearly, Josiah wasn't able to reunite with the baby. I want to find her—Beatrix. I *have* to find her."

"And that's where my online skills and I come in," Amanda said. "I can help. I can try, anyway."

Mel nodded. "Thanks, Amanda. This is personal for me on two counts. As you know, I'm going to *be* an Abernathy. And as I said when I first told you about all this, I *know* and adore Winona—she lives near my parents—she's wonderful but definitely is delicate. She used to be the town psychic and was often written off as an oddball." She shook her head. "She's not doing too well these days. And Josiah is in a nursing home with Alzheimer's. Can you imagine how surprised Gabe and I were when, in a moment of absolute lucidity, Josiah remembered his baby and asked me and Gabe to find her? But I can't so I'm seriously hoping that with your online skills, your sleuthing will find her. The baby was likely born in Rust Creek Falls over seventy years ago and then given up for adoption."

"And Josiah didn't say anything in the diary that might help locate her?" Amanda asked.

"No. All I have on that end is the letter that was tucked inside. I can recite that verbatim. It said, 'My dearest Winona, please forgive me. But they say you will never get better. I promise you that your baby daughter is safe. She's alive! I wanted to raise her myself, but my parents forced me to have her placed for adoption. She's with good people—my parents don't know, but I have figured out who they are. Someday, I will find a way to bring her back to you.'"

Amanda felt tears poke the backs of her eyes. "Oh, Mel. We have to find that baby girl!"

Mel nodded. "We have to. I'm not saying a word to Winona about it until her long-lost daughter is found—if she's found. But I just know this is important."

"I'll do everything I can to find a connection," Amanda said, already thinking how she could go about it. Time frames, hospitals, adoption agencies. Even putting out a general feeler could bring forth leads.

Mel bit her lip. "One major reason why I haven't gotten anywhere is because the psychiatric institution where Winona was sent in Kalispell burned down forty years ago. I wish I had more for you to go on."

Amanda frowned. If the records were gone, then so was any information about why Winona had been sent to that place and details about the baby. Finding Beatrix Abernathy would definitely be harder. She grabbed her phone. "I want to input all of this into my notes app again while it's all fresh in my mind, especially the letter you recited. Can you repeat it—slowly?"

Mel did, and again Amanda's heart clenched with Josiah's clear love for Winona and his determination to reunite with her and their baby girl.

"And you know what else is interesting about the story, Amanda? It seems like everyone who's had something to do with the diary has been truly touched by the story. Hey, who knows? Maybe the diary will bring some romance into your life.

If anyone had told me that after all Gabriel Abernathy and I had been through that we would actually end up engaged…"

Holt Dalton flashed into Amanda's mind. There was no way their brief reunion, even with a future meeting for the interview and photos for the Happy Hearts website, would go anywhere. Because Amanda wouldn't let it. Love—the love she'd felt for Holt, the love she'd felt for Tyler—meant eventually hurting in a way she couldn't bear to go through again. Twice burned, quadruply shy. If *that* wasn't a saying, it should be.

Amanda smiled. "Well, I don't know about that, Mel, but I've got a whole night to see what I can do with my social media skills. I'll be discreet and put out some feelers. I'll keep it to surnames only for a start and see what it leads to."

"Perfect. Thanks, Amanda." Her phone pinged. "Gah. Being CFO of a company means always being on duty. Couple fires to put out, and I'm supposed to be heading out to the party at DJ's. Brittany already leave?"

Amanda nodded. "Yup, you know she likes to be the first on scene of every event she runs."

"Thank God for Brittany. Thanks again, Amanda. See you, Poindexter," she added to the cat, who stood beside Amanda staring up at Mel.

Amanda smiled and shut the door. The documentary on Montana could wait. She had a very interesting mystery to help solve. That would keep her mind off Holt Dalton for sure. For a little while anyway.

Her phone pinged with a text, and she was sure it would be Mel with something she wanted to add about the Winona and Josiah mystery. But it was Holt Dalton.

Got your number from Happy Hearts. I could really use your help. Oliver ran under Robby's bed when we got home and now Bentley's under there too and Robby's worried they both hate him and his room. Robby keeps asking if that "nice Amanda" can come talk to them. Can she? P.S. Sorry if this is way out of bounds. I'll understand.

She swallowed. Oh boy.

Dalton's Grange, right? she texted back. She quickly called it up on her maps app. All the time, the past year, he was right there. I can be over in fifteen minutes.

You're a lifesaver. Log cabin with the bright blue door a half mile back from the main house, nestled in the woods. Tire swing hanging from the big oak out front. Can't miss it.

See you soon, she texted back.

Appreciate it. He added an emoji of a smiley face in a cowboy hat.

She stared at the cowboy smiley face. *Careful, girl*, she told herself. *This is not a guy to be trusted. Don't let a cute kid and two animals you've loved since they came into Happy Hearts get you overinvolved with Holt Dalton.*

Cowboy heartbreaker extraordinaire.

Chapter Three

When the doorbell rang, Oliver was still under the bed—way under—and so was Bentley. Robby was in tears, lying on the floor, head smushed in the crook of his elbow as he'd long given up trying to coax them out.

"Hey, Robby," Holt said. "I'll bet that's Amanda. Want to come to the door with me?"

Robby lifted his head. "I'll wait here. I don't want Bentley and Oliver to think I went away."

Holt nodded and went to the door, barely able to believe that when he opened it, Amanda Jenkins would be standing there. The woman he'd never forgotten.

He'd thought a ringing doorbell would have brought at least Bentley barking and running, but nope, he'd tried that ten minutes ago, and Bentley had stayed put, silent as could be next to his buddy.

Holt opened the door—and whoa. Despite being ten years older, Amanda, in a casual summer outfit of white jeans and a black tank top with a ruffle down the center, looked so much like the girl he'd loved. She wore flat silver sandals, and her toenails were painted a sparkly pink. Her long, lush hair was in a low ponytail, her neck and shoulders exposed. She was so pretty—and sexy.

"Thanks for coming out," Holt said.

"I have to admit, I stood on your porch for a good five minutes staring at the cabin and then up at the main house and the property," she said. "*Wow* does not do Dalton's Grange justice."

The property was definitely spectacular. When his dad said he'd found their ranch, a place for all of them to build the cattle empire they'd always talked about, Holt hadn't expected this. Nestled into the mountains, the main house, which looked like a log mansion, caught his breath every time he passed it. His own house, a miniature version of the main house but still large and comfortable for him and his son—and now a dog and cat—had instantly felt like home. Holt had always been a cowboy through and through, and the log cabin, upscale though it was with its floor-to-ceiling stone fireplace and expert craftsmanship, spoke to him.

"It's so peaceful," he said. "When my head is about to explode, I just have to look up and take in all this wilderness, the mountains, the trees, the cattle, and I can breathe again."

"Is your head often about to explode?"

He nodded.

She stared at him for a moment. "Then I'm glad all you have to do is look around you. Other than try to find peace in a lot more destructive or expensive ways."

"Daddy, is that Amanda?" Robby called out. "Can she come to talk to Bentley and Oliver?"

"Aww," she said. "They're still under the bed, huh?"

"Yup." He gestured for her to come in, and she followed him into the hall, looking all around. "Wow again. This place is incredible. I love everything. It's so wide open yet cozy at the same time."

He watched her take in the vaulted wood ceilings and arched doorways, the warm, colorful rugs and the big leather sofas in the living room, the grand, curved stairway with its tribal treads and photo gallery covering the wall all the way up. "Robby's room is upstairs."

"Four brothers," she said, eyeing the photos of him, Morgan, Boone, Dale and Shep over the years. "I guess the family must have expanded a lot in the past ten years. How many cousins does Robby have?"

"None. My brothers are all single and seem to like it that way. And my ex was an only so no cousins for Robby on that side, either."

"Well, in time I guess the Dalton brothers will settle down. You're so lucky to have a big family. I'm an only myself, as you know, and my parents were onlies, and both sets of grandparents are gone. My parents are all I have, but they retired to Arizona so I don't see them as often I'd like."

"Thanksgiving must be quiet," he said.

She nodded. "Last year my folks went on a cruise with their bridge group, so I was on my own. Luckily, my roommate Brittany invited me over to her family celebration. She's also one of five. I don't think I've ever seen a turkey that big before."

Huh. He was glad she had a kind roommate who looked out for her, but to be alone on Thanksgiving had to hurt. Christmas probably wasn't a blast either.

"Daddy?" Robby called, his voice choked.

"I'm here with Amanda," he called out as he arrived in the doorway of Robby's room. His son had a great bedroom with all his favorite things—lots of hunter green, his favorite color, a shelf devoted to his favorite book series about an amateur detective raccoon in a Hawaiian shirt who solved light, funny mysteries at school, and now Bentley and Oliver's shared bed, which Happy Hearts had wanted Robby to have, and all their toys.

"Hi, Robby," Amanda said, stepping in. "When I brought my cat Poindexter home for the first time after adopting him, he wouldn't come out from under my bed for over four hours."

Robby's eyes widened. "Really? But you're nice."

She sat down beside him. "So are you. It's not that Oliver and Bentley don't like you and aren't happy to be here. They do and are. But animals, particularly cats, get very nervous when they move into a new home. Nothing smells familiar. So they tend to hide under a bed or table until they feel more at home. Then they come out and do a little exploring. Bentley is braver but he's keeping his buddy company so Oliver feels safer."

Robby's face brightened. "That's what Daddy said."

Amanda smiled. "Your daddy is definitely right. So, Robby, why don't you hang out on the rug and just play with a toy or read or whatever you usually do in your room, and I'll bet Oliver comes out to explore. Bentley will be right behind him."

Robby started reaching for his stuffed animals. "I can set up a party of my stuffed animals and toys so that when Bentley and Oliver come out, they can meet everyone."

"That sounds good, Robby," Holt said. He turned to Amanda. "I was about to make some coffee. Sound good?"

"Sure," she said.

"We'll be in the kitchen, Robby. Call down if they come out."

"'Kay, Daddy," Robby said, the anticipation of that in his voice a relief compared to the teary sadness of earlier.

Holt ran a hand over Robby's hair, and Amanda smiled at the boy, then they went downstairs into the kitchen.

"Even the kitchen is gorgeous," she said, looking all around the room. "How does it manage to look antique and state-of-the-art at the same time?"

"Right? Even I don't mind cooking since I moved in."

"*Can* you cook?"

"Hell yeah, I can. For a while there after our

summer at camp, I didn't know what to do with myself. I was always a cowboy, working as a hand, but the places that took a chance on me didn't pay much, so I supplemented my income as a short order cook, thanks to my brief experience in the kitchen at Camp KidPower. Turned out I could make a cheap cut of anything tender and delicious."

"What do you mean you didn't know what to do with yourself?" she asked, clearly confused. "You were in college, majoring in agricultural development, right? You were planning to run a ranching empire."

He moved over to the coffee maker. "I dropped out of school after two years, Amanda. And the summer job at KidPower was court-ordered stupid trouble with the law, petty stuff, disorderly conduct, drinking in public, drag racing, that kind of thing. My life had been going nowhere fast at twenty-two. Till that summer I met you turned me around."

She stared at him, disbelief and resignation in her pretty brown eyes. "Why didn't you tell me?"

He hesitated at first. Then just blurted it out. Finally. "You seemed to like me as I was and I didn't want to spoil it by letting you know I was a hooligan, as my dad used to call me."

She seemed to think about that for a moment.

"You liked me as I was, so I get it. A lot of guys found me boring and thought I was stuck up."

"Shy for sure. Only until someone gets to know you. Then you never stop talking." He grinned, and so did she, and just like that, the ice was broken. Whatever residual anger she'd been holding on to the past ten years seemed to have dissipated. Or maybe that was just wishful thinking on his part.

The relief that hit him was a surprise.

"Well, I wish you'd told me, Holt. I wouldn't have liked you any less."

He wasn't so sure of that.

"Speaking of your father," she added, "I'm surprised you live on the same property with your folks. I remember you saying you and your dad didn't see eye to eye."

Whenever he had opened up to Amanda, he'd been honest. He'd omitted quite a lot, yes, but it had helped back then to talk about his fraught relationship with his dad.

The coffee finally brewed, giving him something to do, somewhere else to look. He poured two mugs, and brought over cream and sugar and sat down across from her.

"No one was more surprised than me," he said. "I still don't get along great with my dad, but I'm working on it. It's my summer plan, actually—to make peace with him. I have barely a month left."

She added cream and a sugar cube to her yellow mug. "Do you argue a lot?"

"I want my father to be someone he's not," he said, taking a long sip of his coffee.

"Sounds like something someone else told you."

He smiled. "All the time. My mother. And all four of my brothers."

"What do you want him to be?" she asked.

"More patient with his grandson." Holt got up and walked over to the counter, where a half-eaten pie sat. "Slice of pecan pie? I made it."

"I never turn down pie," she said. "Especially homemade."

He cut them both a slice and sat back down. Why had he brought up the issue with his dad and Robby? Now he had no appetite for the pie, which he'd only thought of in the first place to have something more to do with himself since the subject of his dad's lack of patience for his grandson grated on him.

"So," she said, taking a bite. "How *does* your dad treat Robby?"

He sighed. "He wants him to stop talking quite so much, stop running quite so fast, stop asking quite so many questions. He wants him to stop being such a whirlwind."

"Too much energy for grandpa?"

He shrugged. "Robby's a great kid. Very energetic, yes. Very talkative, yes. Doesn't always listen, yes. Clumsy as heck, yes. He's seven. He's a lot, I know that."

"Does your father yell at Robby?" she asked, sipping her coffee.

"He's more just gruff. My mother more than makes up for it, but it rankles me. I know my son is a handful, but my dad would be annoyed by any kid who wasn't like a church mouse."

Holt often thought that maybe he should pack Robby up and leave. But the whole reason Holt was here was for his mom. Deborah Dalton had given up so much of herself—including a career she cared about—to help her husband with his dream of having his own ranch, a small place they'd bought in Whitehorn after they'd gotten married. Worrying with him over taxes and cattle prices falling. Up before the crack of dawn to make breakfast, to muck out the barns and stalls, to do just as much heavy lifting. Had his dad appreciated it? Did men who appreciated their wives cheat on them?

No.

A familiar hot pit of anger rose in his gut as he

thought about it. He wouldn't even know about this—and hell, he wished he didn't—if he hadn't overheard an argument as a kid. Another as a teenager. Once, a few years ago, he'd seen his dad standing a little too close to an interested-looking woman in a bar, and Holt had left, feeling sick. Before they'd ever moved to Bronco, when his mom was recovering from the heart attack that had scared them all, he'd overheard his dad talking to the hospital chaplain, asking forgiveness for not loving his wife right or good enough, admitting he'd cheated and making a solemn vow to never betray his marriage vows again. His father had been crying, and Holt had retreated, bursting into tears himself.

He could count on his hands the times he'd cried as an adult—when he'd walked away from Amanda ten years ago, not sure why he was so upset over something *he* was actually doing. When the divorce papers arrived. When his son was placed in his arms for the first time less than a minute after he was born. And that day he'd overheard his father with the chaplain.

Amanda took another bite of the pie. "I guess your family chose Bronco for the same reason I did. And most folks. It's pretty great here. The Wild West, the old ghost legends, downtown Bronco Heights. I love it here."

"I do too. So does Robby. When the ranch in Whitehorn failed, my dad was thinking of moving to Rust Creek Falls, where we have a lot of family, but our branch didn't exactly have a good reputation then, so my dad just said Rust Creek Falls was too small town for his taste and that Bronco had everything we could want. He got lucky gambling, which was how he was able to afford this place. And because we know my dad has a penchant for letting good things slip away, we all moved to the ranch at my mother's request to make sure the place runs smoothly and to keep an eye on our mom, who'd had a heart attack not long before."

He'd never forget how he'd ended up here with his dad—how all his brothers had. Their first night in Bronco, sitting around the big dining table in their huge new dining room, his father had said he had his own personal kind of grace to say and went on to announce that he'd been lucky a few times in his life. The first was when Deborah had agreed to marry him despite him having not a nickel to his name. The second was when he won the money to give her the life she deserved. When Neal had brought Dalton's Grange, he'd asked his sons, scattered across Montana working on other ranches, to come work for him, assuring them there were houses on the property for all of them to live separately if they wanted. All five Dalton brothers refused. But then their mother asked them to reconsider. She wanted her family together, a true second chance for them all. How could they possibly refuse after what she'd gone through?

"Is she doing all right?" Amanda asked.

"Good as gold," he said. "But we almost lost her and none of us had ever been so scared."

"So the seven of you got to start fresh in Bronco. Like me."

"Like you?" he asked, raising an eyebrow. He should have figured something had made her leave Whitehorn, besides just her parents retiring and leaving themselves.

She frowned and then dug into her pie, clearly not wanting to talk about it. He got it. There was a lot he didn't want to talk about either.

"There are some other prosperous ranching families who aren't so welcoming," he said. "I guess we're considered 'new money' without a family history or legacy in town. And a little rough around the edges to say the least."

She smiled. "Well, if you're rough around the edges, Holt Dalton, you're a diamond in the rough. I spent a lot of time with you ten years ago, even for just a summer, and there's nothing rough about you."

Without thinking, he reached out for her hand and gave it a gentle squeeze. "That's nice of you to say."

"Daddy! Amanda! Come look!"

Amanda's smile lit up her face. "I have a feeling a certain cat and dog have come out from under the bed."

They both took one last sip of their coffees, then went upstairs, stopping in the doorway to Robby's room, mostly because Holt was so surprised. Robby was sitting cross-legged on the rug in front of the fancy memory-foam pet bed, where Bentley and Oliver were lying down, Oliver curled up along Bentley's belly.

Robby was reading from a chapter book, "'And then…'" He stopped and put his finger on the page. "'And then Rocco…'" He bit his lip, moving his finger to the right. "'Rocco the raccoon said…'" He moved his finger and stared down hard at the page. "'Well, that.'" He stopped and shifted his body a bit. "'Well that sure is…is a mystery!'" He looked up at his pets with a smile. "Bentley and Oliver, I know that word by heart now! Mystery! Isn't that a big word? It means something that no one can figure out." He looked back down at the page. "'But don't worry, I can…'" He stared at the page, his face scrunching in concentration. He turned around and looked at Holt. "Daddy? What is this word again?"

Holt came in the room and glanced at where Robby pointed. "Solve. Do you remember what that means?"

Robby nodded. "That's the figuring out part, right?"

Holt nodded. "You got it, Robby."

The boy continued reading. "'But don't worry,'" he said again, "'I can solve it!'" Robby glanced up from his book at Bentley and Oliver. "Guys, don't worry about the missing chalk in the classroom because Rocco the raccoon is really good at solving mysteries!"

Amanda moved beside Holt. "Oh, my heart," she whispered to him. "He is the sweetest."

Holt smiled at her, holding her gaze a beat longer than he should have, but he could barely drag his eyes off her. "Good job, buddy," he said to his son.

"Do you think Bentley and Oliver like being read to even by me?" Robby asked, his blue eyes worried and his mouth kind of scrunched up.

"I can tell they love it," Amanda said. "Look at how calm they are. They seem very happy you're reading to them."

Robby brightened. "I'm not a good reader, though. I'm in the worst group at school. But maybe I'll get better if I read to Bentley and Oliver."

"That would be great practice," Amanda said with a nod.

The doorbell rang, and Holt excused himself to answer it, his heart in his throat as it often was when Robby opened up about his struggles with reading. A glance out the window showed his dad's pickup in the drive. Great. His father was here with some complaint, probably about how Robby was running too close to the bulls pasture this morning and it wasn't good for them.

But it was Holt's mother on the porch with a red bag in her hand. *Bronco Pets Emporium* was in gold across the bag.

"Special delivery for Robby Dalton," she said with a smile. Tall like all the Daltons but with short blond hair cut to her chin and warm blue eyes like Robby's, Deborah held out the bag.

He gave his mom a kiss on the cheek. "That was nice of you, Mom."

"And your dad too," she added quickly. "He's the one who drove us into town to the pet shop. Even tested out the squeaker in Bentley's new toy."

"Thanks for the warning," Holt said with a smile, hating the loud squeakers. "Dad not here too?" he asked, glancing past her into the truck.

Empty. He'd let his parents know he'd adopted not only the dog he'd promised Robby but a cat, and that they'd both stay in the house, not roam around loose.

"He's rolling out the dough for pizza night, actually," she said. "The man can't cook but he likes to roll out the dough."

Holt had definitely gotten his skills in the kitchen from his mother, who was a great cook. His father managed to scorch pots of spaghetti, always letting the water boil out because he completely forgot he was cooking in the first place. Deborah had pretty much banned him from their state-of-the-art kitchen.

"Come on upstairs," Holt said. "Robby just managed to coax his pets out from under his bed, so your timing is perfect. Oh, and I have a visitor— Amanda Jenkins. We worked at that summer camp together ten years ago. Turns out she does social media for Happy Hearts, and I ran into her there earlier today."

He did catch the look of surprise and curiosity on his mom's face. When was the last time he'd brought a woman into his home? Not this year, certainly.

They'd reached Robby's bedroom, and his mom walked in quietly so as not to scare the pets. She looked at Amanda and smiled, then turned to her grandson. "Robby, I have a happy-new-pets present for you!"

Robby's face lit up. "Thanks, Gram!" He stood slowly as if he knew any sudden movements would send Oliver racing back under the bed. He opened the gifts and again, it might as well have been Christmas morning. "A stuffed rabbit for Bentley and a catnip mouse for Oliver!"

Deborah grinned. "We also got Oliver his own cat condo so he has a place to scratch and climb and get high up the way cats like. That's in the car. Holt, you can bring it up before I go. And we got Bentley his very own indoor doghouse. It's made out of sturdy foam and has a cushy bed."

The trip to the pet store and all the gifts might have been his mom's idea, but his dad certainly hadn't vetoed it. His father was overly generous with his wife, especially, but his sons and Robby too. If he had it, he'd share it. That had always been his dad's way.

"That was above and beyond," Holt said. "Thank you."

"You're the best gram in the whole entire world!" Robby said, propelling himself at his grandmother for a hug.

She laughed and wrapped her arms around him, then looked at Amanda.

"Mom, this is Amanda Jenkins," he said.

"Amanda, my mother, Deborah Dalton. I was just telling my mom that we met in camp all those years ago and ran into each other at Happy Hearts."

"Isn't that something," his mother said. "Such a small world. Amanda, why don't you stay for dinner tonight? It'll be ready in about thirty minutes. I have this fancy brick-oven-style contraption in the kitchen, so how could I not use it on everyone's favorite food?"

Amanda bit her lip and glanced at Holt. Was she looking for help getting out of the invitation? Thing was, if she did want him to give her an easy excuse, he didn't want to.

He wanted her to stay.

"Yay, Amanda is having dinner with us!" Robby said with absolutely no assurance of that and shooting her a big smile. "Gram, Amanda helped us at Happy Hearts. She's so nice."

"She certainly is," Holt said, hoping she'd say yes. "I hope you can stay, Amanda. Unless you have plans." There—he'd provided her the out.

Don't take it, he willed her. *Don't say, "Well, actually, I do have plans, sorry."* She probably would say that—and not even add "another time."

Because from the look on her pretty face, she didn't want there to be another time.

After how he'd treated her ten years ago, who

could blame her? Even if he had explained himself. Maybe the truth was worse than the crime
itself, despite what she'd said in the kitchen a little while ago. He hadn't been anyone she'd have
wanted to be involved with.

"I'd love to," she said, surprising him and getting a hug from Robby, who'd gotten up again
and wrapped his arms around her. Amanda
laughed. "Thanks for the invitation," she said to
his mother. "Can I help?"

"Oh no, you enjoy your visit with Holt and
Robby," Deborah said. "But thank you."

"I'm going to teach Oliver and Bentley tricks,"
Robby said, getting back down on the floor to tell
them about pizza night and how Gram always
made his favorite, half pepperoni, half mushroom.
Robby loved mushrooms on everything.

Holt could give his mother and son five hugs
each. They'd gotten Amanda to stay for dinner.
That he didn't want their time to end registered
loud and clear. He wanted to get to know this new,
older Amanda. But he could see from her expression that she was very wary of him. Maybe that
was a good thing. Yeah, it probably was. He had a
lot on his plate. His work on the ranch, which kept
him busy. Almost a full month of summer left
without childcare or camps, thanks to the camp
director making him feel Robby wasn't welcome.

And this thing with his dad, which had come to a head last week when Robby was doing his chore of feeding his beloved chickens. His father had told Holt that Robby had let one of them get out and if it happened again, his son would be banned from the coop.

Holt had stood up for Robby—the boy was seven and chickens were sneaky. Seemed like his dad was always complaining about something; it was the Neal Dalton way. Holt had barely spoken to his father the past few weeks, mostly because Holt was keeping his distance. But his mom had specifically asked him to come tonight since all the Dalton brothers were attending.

Now tonight he'd have to deal with his dad *and* having Amanda Jenkins back in his life— and he didn't know what the next steps were in dealing with either.

Chapter Four

Amanda had never been inside a log mansion—
and boy, was she glad she'd changed out of her
yoga pants, long tank and owl socks when she'd
first been asked over to Holt's and into something
presentable for an unexpected family dinner. The
gorgeous main house at Dalton's Grange went on
forever, sprawling against the mountains. The
home was a lot like Holt's much smaller version,
vaulted wood ceilings, huge windows, arched
doorways, a floor-to-ceiling stone fireplace and
rustic-luxe furnishings. The dining room alone
was almost twice the size of Amanda's big bed-

room at BH247. Then again, with eight Daltons living on the property, Amanda supposed they'd need a big dining space for when they all got together.

The polished wood table also went on forever, comfortably seating everyone. Holt and Amanda were across from each other at the center of the table, Robby beside his father and next to his uncle Morgan. The oldest at thirty-four, Morgan was as blond and blue-eyed as Holt was dark-haired and dark-eyed, though the family resemblance was easily seen in the shape of the eyes, the nose, even their expressions. Holt was second oldest at thirty-two. Thirty-year-old Boone was somewhere in between, coloring-wise. Rounding out the Dalton siblings were Shep and Dale, both in their twenties, who lived in the house with Neal and Deborah. Amanda had felt eyes on her constantly when she'd first been introduced to the Dalton men. The siblings all had teasing grins on their faces for Holt, who apparently wasn't one to bring a woman home for dinner. Neal had welcomed her kindly and made some small talk about Whitehorn, which he said he didn't miss one bit.

As Amanda helped herself to a slice of roasted vegetable pizza, which looked delicious, she gazed around the table, the Daltons all chatting away about the ranch and a runaway horse, who'd

been caught eventually, and then talk turned to
Bentley and Oliver. Before Deborah had left
Holt's house earlier, Amanda and Holt had carried up the indoor doghouse and cat condo. Oliver
had explored his new catnip-scented playhouse
immediately and seemed to love the high perch.
Bentley had gone inside his doghouse, which
Robby had festooned with toys, but since Oliver
had seemed content enough, the dog had jumped
up on Robby's bed, turned around three times,
and then settled down with a happy sigh. Robby
had hugged his grandmother again and again,
beside himself with happiness.

Amanda already adored the kid. She'd used
the rest of the time before dinner to interview
Holt and Robby for the Happy Hearts website and
take photos. In addition to photos of little Robby
and his new pets, she now had one too many pictures of Holt Dalton on her phone. Available to
ogle anytime.

As Robby talked more and more about his new
pets, his grandfather, sitting at the head of the
table, seemed to be a bit irritated by his grandson. Robby was talking a mile a minute, answering his uncle's questions, and Holt was focused
on their conversation.

Amanda hadn't been sure if Holt had been
overstating his father's impatience with Robby

in his own anger over it. Given Neal's frustrated expression as he glanced at Robby, Holt hadn't been exaggerating. Neal, in his sixties with salt-and-pepper hair, tall and muscular like his sons, was now having a completely separate conversation with his son Dale, who sat to his left.

At the other end of the table, Deborah asked Robby questions about Bentley and Oliver, the boy excitedly answering.

"Gramps, will you come meet Bentley and Oliver too?" Robby asked. "Everyone's coming over after dinner to meet them."

All eyes were on Gramps. Amanda noticed Deborah Dalton's blue gaze was fierce on her husband, daring him to make an excuse.

"Sure I'm coming," Neal said with a smile at Robby—a genuine smile.

Robby beamed and reached for another slice of pepperoni and mushroom.

Amanda glanced at Holt. Whew. There was hope here. Neal could have said no, that he was tired, but he clearly did care deeply about his grandson.

As dinner went on, with so much talking and laughing, folks from each side asking her questions about living in downtown Bronco Heights and if she thought social media was going to be the downfall of global society—that one came from Holt's dad, of course—Amanda felt herself growing more and more wistful. Dinner growing up in the Jenkins family certainly hadn't been like this. With three shy Jenkinses at the table, no one had said much of anything. Every now and then, one of them would bring up something light and then go back to chewing and dabbing his or her mouth. Amanda had always figured it was the reason she'd become such a bookworm: reading allowed her to inhabit other worlds, be a part of the story, the family in the book. She got to be both Fern and Wilbur in *Charlotte's Web* and Anne and Anne's best friend, Diana, in *Anne of Green Gables*, and in all the romances and mysteries she read now, she got to be all different kinds of heroines. Being here at Dalton's Grange reminded her of being in a very good book.

Amanda had gone to quite a few gatherings that Brittany invited her to, forcing herself to be social, but she felt so out of place, wishing that piping up with an interesting thing to say came easily. Tonight, she found herself talking easily with this crew. They were a warm, welcoming bunch, even if Neal Dalton had too much of the "get off my lawn" at the ready.

"So, dessert at my house," Holt said, glancing around the table at his family. "I whipped up three pies this morning. Well, four, but I'm almost through one already."

"Daddy is the best cook," Robby said. "After Gram," he added quickly.

Deborah laughed. "I'd like to think I taught your daddy everything he knows about the kitchen."

"Why didn't it rub off on me?" Morgan asked, stealing a pepperoni off the edge of a pizza and popping it into his mouth.

As the brothers ribbed one another, again Amanda wished she had a family like this. Close, loving, sharing a weekday meal because they happened to live very close by and because they loved one another.

As they all headed out to walk in the gorgeous night air down to Holt's cabin, Amanda whispered, "I'll leave when we get to your house. I don't want to intrude any more than I have already."

Holt stopped in his tracks. "And miss my chocolate cream pie? My lemon chiffon? Are you kidding me?"

That was how Amanda ended up staying for dessert, sitting on the big leather chair by the fireplace and watching as Holt's brothers made a fuss over Bentley. Oliver had come as far as the stairs and refused to go farther, but Amanda was sure he'd warm enough to the house by tomorrow. Holt had set out the pies and plates and forks on the buffet in the living room, and had brought out the coffee maker, which made individual cups. The Daltons were again eating and sipping and talking and laughing, Amanda loving being part of this big rowdy crew.

But then Robby tried to see if Bentley knew how to play fetch, which meant grabbing a remote control and tossing it across the room, which hit a lamp and knocked it over, and Neal Dalton had an absolute fit.

"Robby! What in the world were you thinking!" Neal said. "You don't throw things! Is a remote control a stick? And you don't throw sticks in the house anyway!"

Robby's eyes got wide and he hung his head, dropping down and burying his face in Bentley's black-and-white fur.

"Dad, tone it down!" Holt said to Neal, holding up a hand. "It was an accident."

"Yes, just an accident," Deborah put in. "Let me get a broom and dustpan."

"I've got it, Mom," Holt said. "Enjoy your coffee."

"Who can enjoy their coffee with glass shards all over the place?" Neal said, shaking his head.

"You had five sons, Dad. You're gonna tell me you're not used to broken lamps? Come on. You've got to lighten up."

Neal frowned. "I'm grumpy because I'm tired." He sent Robby something of a smile, then got up and headed to the door. "Come on, Deborah. We both have to get up early."

"It's okay, Mom," Holt whispered.

Deborah kissed Holt on the cheek. "The pie was delicious." She looked at Amanda. "Lovely to meet you, Amanda."

The parents were suddenly gone, and then the brothers all headed to the door within minutes. "Don't mind Grumpy Gramps, Robby," Morgan said to his nephew.

"Seriously, Robby," Boone said, running a hand through his nephew's tousled hair, "Gramps didn't mean to yell. He's just tired from a long day with a sick bull."

"Yeah?" Holt asked. "Bull okay?"

Boone nodded. "He'll be fine. Dad stayed with him most of the day and once the meds kicked in, he was better."

"Hey, Robby," Dale said. "I once threw the TV remote at Shep's head when he was making fun of me for something in middle school, and it knocked over Gramp's favorite coffee mug that was on an end table. He lit into me for a good ten minutes and grounded me for a year but he was mad at something else, not me. Mom said he'd gotten a huge tax bill that day and his patience level was at zero."

"I remember that," Shep said. "And your aim is still terrible by the way."

Robby laughed. "So Gramps isn't really mad at me?"

"Nah," Holt assured his son. "An accident is an accident, right? You didn't mean to knock over the lamp. But you did break it because you were playing fetch in the house. Next time you want to play fetch with Bentley, you have to go outside. Understood?"

"Yes, Daddy," he said, wrapping Holt in a hug.

"And don't use a remote control, Robby," Holt added. "Use Uncle Morgan's shoe instead."

"I'll get you," Morgan said with a grin, fake punching Holt in the gut.

Robby laughed.

Amanda felt tears poke the backs of her eyes. Could this family be any lovelier?

Suddenly, it was just three of them. Bentley and Oliver had *long* come out from under the bed, the whole reason she'd come over in the first place. They'd eaten dinner. They'd had dessert. But Amanda didn't want to leave.

Holt had to somehow prolong Amanda's time in the house, so when Robby asked her to read him a bedtime story, he could not have been more grateful to his son.

"Sure, Robby," Amanda said. She seemed to like that she was a little kid's favorite new person in the world.

Back up in Robby's room, Amanda pulled over the desk chair by his bed while Holt sank down in the easy chair by the window. He'd read his son countless books over the past seven years, starting when he was just two days old and home from the hospital. Sally Anne, Robby's mother, had been rightfully tired, but as time passed, she'd never seemed comfortable feeding him or giving him his bath or taking care of him in the middle of the night. So Holt had done all that. He'd taken to fatherhood so easily because he loved Robby from the moment he knew about him. He and Sally Anne might have always had their problems, but ever since she'd told him she was pregnant, he was madly in love with his child.

Robby was a mini Holt, too, except for the eye color. He'd gotten his mother's baby blues but the rest was all Holt.

"'*Rocco and the Case of the Missing Chocolate Cake*,'" Amanda read, holding up the cover for Robby to see. His bedtime story was always a few chapters from a Rocco the Raccoon mystery.

"Yay, I love that one," Robby said. He'd asked

Amanda to pick out one from his favorites shelf. He yawned and pulled the blanket up to his chin.

Holt had no doubt he'd be asleep by chapter two. "Night, buddy," he said. "Just in case you fall asleep while Amanda's still reading."

"Night, Daddy. Night, Bentley. Night, Oliver."

Oliver was on the top perch of his kitty condo, which seemed his favorite place in the room. Bentley was sprawled across the foot of Robby's bed as if he'd always been part of the family. Holt could barely believe they'd just brought these two home *today*.

Bentley lifted his head, tilting it that adorable way dogs did, then closed his eyes. Amanda started reading.

"Oh wait. Good night, Amanda," Robby said. "Thanks for reading to me."

"Good night, Robby. And it's my pleasure."

Robby's eyes drooped with every word Amanda read. She'd gotten to page three, which was the end of chapter one, when Robby was clearly asleep.

"And my work here is done," she whispered with a smile.

"Hope not," he said. "I thought I could tempt you to stay for a cup of coffee. Dessert got kind of interrupted earlier."

"Sounds good," she said. Warily.

I'm more scared of you than you are of me, he wanted to tell her. *I might have hurt you ten years ago, but I'm not in a place to fall for someone. Or to get kicked to the curb.* But there was no way he was backing away from what he was feeling. Which was simply wanting to be with Amanda.

Downstairs in the kitchen, he brewed more coffee and suggested taking it out to the back deck so that Bentley could go out for a while. Amanda said something about the weather and the moon being gorgeous tonight, but he really had eyes only for her. It was just like the first time he'd seen her and had been so struck by a feeling—not just attraction but a feeling of *rightness.* He didn't know what that had meant at the time or even now, but when he looked at Amanda Jenkins, everything about his world felt right. Over the past few years that he'd been on his own, a single guy, he'd gone on dates his brothers had set up for him or with women who'd asked him out in the bakery aisle of the grocery store or in the pickup line at school, and half the time, he felt like they were on different planets. Lack of connection, of chemistry. With Amanda, it just felt *right*.

He went upstairs and whispered to Bentley to come, which the good boy did immediately, then the two joined Amanda on the deck. Holt set down the mugs of coffee on the table between their chaises, then stretched out, watching the border collie explore the backyard and sniff every blade of grass.

"Sorry you had to be there for that awkwardness with my dad and Robby," Holt said. Granted, Robby had done wrong and been wrong, but for his grandfather to yell like that—Holt didn't like it. Rage might make people, particularly kids, fearful, but it certainly wouldn't turn an impulsive kid into a more thoughtful, careful one.

"Well, I got to see firsthand what you meant," Amanda said, crossing her long legs at the ankles and picking up her coffee. "About your dad's lack of patience. I like how you handled it—explaining why it was wrong, that it was wrong. But it was an accident."

Holt ran a hand over his face. "I'm glad you said that. Half the time I don't know if I'm being too easy on him or if I just get him."

"Thank God you get him, Holt. Why do you think you're his hero?"

A warmth started in his gut and traveled straight up to his chest, left side. Damn. She got *him*. "I almost forgot you heard all that at the Happy Hearts. When he was talking to the cow."

She smiled. "I still can't get over saying 'how sweet' thinking I was talking to a complete stranger and finding the—" She stopped talking, watching Bentley intently as he explored the large yard.

"The guy who acted like a heartless jerk to the woman he loved," he finished for her.

"Well, you definitely didn't love me, Holt. Or you wouldn't have walked away."

He shook his head. "At the time I walked away because I *did* love you. I know that sounds nuts. You were the first person to treat me like I was not only worth something, but special. Almost like a golden boy—me." He shook his head, hardly able to believe anyone thought he was that guy. "Guys who had everything."

"You *were* that guy, Holt. I didn't create you. I met you and got to know you and fell in love with exactly what was in front of me. You."

Huh. He'd never thought of it that way. Certainly not back then. He'd been so sure she'd never accept the "real him," and he didn't have the heart to test out his theory. So he'd said something awful about being a rolling stone and wished her well. He'd never forget the look on her face. The confusion, the betrayal, and what she'd said about forgetting how people could shock you. And his own anguish at the time was something he'd never stopped carrying with him.

"I'm surprised you didn't become a teacher

for kids with special needs," he said, wanting to change the subject.

She sipped her coffee. "That was my plan, but turns out that in college, during my fieldwork of observation and student teaching at an elementary school, I was so shy I couldn't speak up or exert myself and I realized I couldn't stand up in front of twenty-five third graders and lead a classroom. I liked learning about education—theories and new practices—but being a teacher required something that I just didn't have and I knew it."

"That must have been rough to discover about yourself," he said. "Was it?"

"Well, it's important to know who you are and figure out where your strengths can take you. For a shy, bookish girl, I was shocked to find out I was good at marketing and social media outreach—promoting all kinds of businesses. I got to shower all my ideas and pep and passion on my work and in my campaigns—it's less about dealing with people than about the campaigns. My work just has to do my talking for me."

"That's really interesting," he said. "How'd you even find out you were good at marketing?"

"I took a marketing class in college and then did an internship at a really luxe dude ranch that celebs and their kids would vacation at. I found my calling—social media in the wilderness of

Montana. I love my job and being surrounded by ranches here in Bronco. Best of both worlds. But I do volunteer at the elementary school. I didn't entirely walk away from education and helping kids. I help out with reading and math for kindergarten through third grade. I've never been assigned to Robby's classroom, though. Dalton isn't that uncommon a name, but it would have stood out for me."

He sat up and turned to face her. "You tutor kids in reading?"

"Sometimes, yes. Why?"

"Would you consider privately tutoring Robby this summer? His confidence is so low. I'd love for him to walk into second grade the very first day knowing that he'll be moved from the 'worst reading group.'" He shook his head that Robby even knew he was in the lowest group.

"Kids are so aware—self aware and aware of others and where they fit in academically and socially. Even in the very early grades. It's awful."

"Yeah. Unless you really *are* a golden boy," he added with a grin. "Then you're on easy street."

"Eh, no one gets away from bad stuff happening," she said.

"True," he said, holding her gaze.

Bentley walked up to the deck and tilted his head as if deciding who to lie next to. He chose the soft mat in between their chairs and stretched out. Holt gave him a scratch and he got a pat from Amanda.

"I'd be happy to work with Robby," she finally said.

He wondered if she'd taken a few moments to respond because she didn't really want to but felt she couldn't say no. She seemed to like Robby—a lot, actually. But he could tell Amanda was ambivalent about spending time with her new student's dad. The one who broke her heart and walked away.

He wanted to ask about her hesitation in saying yes, but he figured he'd just accept that she *had* said yes and not look the ole gift horse in the mouth. "I'll warn you," he said. "He's not easy. He gets distracted and bored and unless he can read Rocco the Raccoon mysteries, he's not too interested in reading. But I'll pay you well." He named a figure that was at least a third more than he'd been quoted by other tutors that hadn't worked out—at all.

"I won't take a cent from you, Holt. Call it the we-have-a-past one-hundred-percent discount." She smiled. "Besides, I really like Robby and already think of him as my little buddy, not a client. He might be a whirlwind chatterbox to others, but I find his energy and excitement life-affirming."

Again, there was that feeling in his chest—warmth, gratitude. "Wow. How'd I get so lucky to have you walk back into my life?"

Oh, crud. The moment the words were out of his mouth he realized he shouldn't have said them. Or quite that way.

She sat up and faced him. "I'll be upfront, Holt. I'm not looking to reunite here."

He stared at her. "I'm not either." He was but he wasn't. He hoped that was what she meant too.

"Good," she said. "Nothing against you or what happened ten years ago," she added. "But I've been through…stuff since. And I'm done with all that."

"All that? You mean dating?"

She glanced away. "Well, I mean love. I'm done with love."

He raised an eyebrow. "You can't be done with love. You can't possibly control it."

She looked him right in the eyes. "You did, remember? You said just a little while ago that despite loving me, you left me."

Oh hell. He did say that. "But it cost me, Amanda. I didn't even realize what a bad state I was in at the time, leaving you like that. Not having you in my life anymore. I wasn't exactly Guy of the Year. And then I met Sally Anne and I thought, okay, she's rough around the edges like me, my kind of woman. She got pregnant by accident, and I'll tell you, Amanda, my life changed in that moment. Every bad habit I had I kicked to the curb. Driving too fast, drinking too much, running wild like I didn't have a care. I *had* a care—a baby. That was it. I changed like that." He snapped his fingers for emphasis.

"But it didn't work out. You and Sally Anne."

He really didn't like thinking back to his marriage. "I was a lot more into making it work than she was. She wasn't even all that interested in marrying me but her parents, who had a lot of problems with her, told her they'd cut her out of the will if she didn't make them respectable grandparents. They didn't have much, but they had enough to make her say I do."

"Oh God, this sounds awful."

"It gets worse." He took a long sip of his cooling coffee. "We got married when I was twenty-five. She was just twenty-two. She'd always told me she wasn't cut out for motherhood and I guess she tried here and there, but she left when Robby was three. When her parents passed away in a car accident, nothing in her life felt right and she moved out to Colorado where she had some friends. And now she sends cards and small gifts for birthdays and Christmas, but that's it. She doesn't come visit."

"Robby must ask about his mom," she asked softly.

"He does. Less now than the first year she left. But he's often reminded of her absence in other ways. You know how it is at school since you volunteer—moms coming in for special class events and choral concerts and to be the guest reader. It's always just me or his grandmother."

Amanda touched a hand to her chest. "Oh, my heart hurts thinking about that."

"Keeps me up at night, Amanda. But that's our life. And we have a good one. Robby has a devoted father, grandparents who love him, uncles who dote on him. Morgan taught Robby to ride a two-wheeler. Boone takes him fishing every Sunday. Dale's the one who got Robby interested in the rodeo and takes him to all Daring Drake's events. And Shep takes Robby hiking up in the mountains, tiring him out good."

"That's wonderful. He's truly lucky to have all of that love."

Holt nodded. "Yeah. It's why I know I made the right decision coming back, working for my dad, hard as it is to be around him so often. I try to keep my distance." He was still sitting facing her, their knees almost touching. He wanted to reach out and touch her face, her hair.

"Did I just tell you my life story?" he asked.

She smiled. "I'm glad you did."

He wasn't sure if he moved forward or if she did, but suddenly their lips met in an unexpected kiss.

"Whoa, cowboy," she said. "How'd we get here?"

"I don't regret it," he said, looking right into her beautiful dark eyes.

"I have to," she said, standing up. "I'm not going there, Holt. I can't. If I help Robby this summer, you have to make me a promise that we'll be platonic. Don't flirt, don't sweet talk me, don't come near me with those lips."

He stood too. "Well, it's not going to be easy but given how crazy my life is right now, I shouldn't be trying to start something with anyone." Especially not the one woman who could bring him to his knees. Sometimes he thought the real reason he left Amanda was because he knew she would have left him if she knew the truth about him, and he wouldn't have been able to survive that pain.

"So we have a deal?" she asked.

"A tough deal, but a deal."

"Shake it on. Cowboy's code means you can't break it."

He smiled and shook, mostly just to feel her hand against his, but inside he was sweating. Because he was already dreaming of breaking that code.

Chapter Five

Ten minutes after Amanda had gotten home from the extended trip to Dalton's Grange, she was back in her jammies and sitting at her desk in front of her laptop, determined to focus on the decades-old mystery of what became of Beatrix Abernathy. If she worked on helping Mel track down the long-lost daughter of the two young separated lovers, Amanda wouldn't think about Holt. Or the kiss. Or the agreement she'd made to tutor his son.

Yet all she was thinking about was the unexpected kiss. Their chemistry was on fire, always had been, so the kiss was no surprise. There was just something between them as there had been from the first day she'd seen Holt Dalton ten years ago at Camp KidPower. And the more he opened up to her about what was really going on in his life, the closer she felt to him. Unfortunately.

She should not, could not feel close to him. Not after how badly he'd hurt her. As she'd told him on the deck, she was done with love, done with opening herself up to heart-wrenching pain. She had to keep some distance from Holt, some-how. His promise to keep his lips to himself was a good start.

Beatrix Abernathy, she told herself, staring at the search engine. Amanda went over her notes in her phone app, reading the words in the letter found tucked between the pages of Josiah Aber-nathy's diary.

My dearest Winona, please forgive me. But they say you will never get better. I promise you that your baby daughter is safe. She's alive! I wanted to raise her myself, but my parents forced me to have her placed for adoption. She's with good people—my par-ents don't know, but I have figured out who they are. Someday, I will find a way to bring her back to you.

Winona Cobbs was in her nineties now. And according to Mel she was delicate and frail these days. They had to fulfill Josiah's promise as quickly as possible—especially now that Josiah had had that moment of remembrance.

I'll do everything I can to help. Amanda sent the promise silently into the universe.

Hmm, Amanda thought, staring at her computer screen. She'd done some marketing work for a hospital and recalled there was an online group of adoptees looking for information about their birth parents. She could start with a group such as that one. But where to focus the search? Winona and her family had lived in Rust Creek Falls back then, where she'd likely given birth.

Since the Abernathys had moved to Bronco after the baby had been adopted, Mel had said she had a feeling the baby had been adopted to a Bronco family. Perhaps, like Josiah, the Abernathys also knew which family the newborn had been placed with and wanted to keep tabs from a distance or just live in the same area with the little girl who wouldn't be part of their own family. Mel hadn't been sure of any of that.

Amanda figured she'd start with online groups related to Rust Creek Falls, a very small town, and Bronco. With Poindexter on her lap, she did some searches for online groups concerning adoption in Kalispell and bingo—there was a public chat group of people looking for information. Amanda typed her own new post into the site:

> I'm looking for information about a baby girl likely born in Rust Creek Falls seventy-plus years ago to teenaged parents and placed for adoption by the birth father's family. The families—the surnames are Cobbs and Abernathy—would have originally been from Rust Creek Falls. I have reason to believe the adoptive family was from Bronco. Please contact me with any leads.

She closed her laptop. Her post was pretty general, but there was a time frame, a place, surnames—and all that was a good start. You never knew what could resonate with someone out there and bring forth a lead.

I hope we find you, Beatrix Abernathy, Amanda thought, giving her cat a few scratches by her tail.

She heard a key in the lock, which meant Brittany was home. Her roommate came in and locked up, then took off her high heels, sighing with relief.

"Ahhh. These pinched me all night. Gorgeous

but painful," she said, wagging her finger at the sexy stilettos.

Amanda sent her a rueful smile. "Just like the guy I spent the past few hours with." She felt her eyes widen as she realized what she'd just blurted out. "Did I just say that?"

Brittany came rushing over to the sofa and plopped down. "What guy? I thought you were spending the evening on the sofa with that documentary." She reached into her purse and pulled out a velvet scrunchie, then pulled her long hair into a low ponytail.

"Well, that was the plan. And then Holt called."

Brittany raised an eyebrow. "Holt? I like that name. Sounds sexy."

"Oh, he is," Amanda said, feeling herself blush. She was very comfortable with Brittany and always felt like she could be herself and say what was on her mind. But she hadn't had a guy to gush about in the two years she'd lived here. Not that Holt was hers. "I've mentioned him, though not by name. He was that summer love ten years ago at a camp where we worked. I thought we'd be together forever, but he dumped me the last day. I ran into him late this afternoon when I was at Happy Hearts to go over some work with Daphne."

"He was at Happy Hearts? Is he a vegan who doesn't wear leather shoes?" she asked.

Amanda laughed. "The opposite. He's a cattle breeder. His family owns one of the biggest and most gorgeous ranches in Bronco Heights—Dalton's Grange."

"He's a Dalton? There are a zillion of them and each one is better looking than the last."

Very true. Holt was the cutest, in Amanda's opinion—then each was cuter than the last. "Five brothers to be exact. And yup, I met them all tonight at dinner at the parents' house. Holt's mother invited me to stay."

"Ooooh," Brittany said. "Tell me every detail."

Amanda did. She left nothing out. Starting with Robby Dalton wanting to adopt a cow and ending with the hot kiss from Holt on the back deck. And the promise they'd both made not to repeat it.

"Oh sure," Brittany said, shaking her head with a grin. "Like *that* will happen. That was some intense evening, Amanda. You two will be lip-locked within minutes of seeing each other the next time."

"He's an *amazing* kisser," Amanda said, biting her lip as she recalled every delicious sensation that had consumed her. "But I mean it. No more. First of all, he completely broke my heart and was careless about it too. He just walked away, Brittany." She'd never told her roommate about getting left at the altar two years ago right before moving to Bronco. When she'd arrived in town, she'd wanted this to be about a fresh start, not re-hashing everything that went wrong in her life, so she'd just said she'd had her share of heartache and wasn't looking to get involved with anyone. "I guess I just don't have faith in love anymore."

"Your trust was shot," Brittany said, her dark eyes sympathetic. "I can understand that. But life and love are about risks."

Poindexter moved and Amanda petted his back and cute head, her gaze on the sweet, loving cat who never gave her any trouble. "That's just it. I don't want to take risks. I never want to be that hurt again. There was a next time with someone else too. I did try again and look what happened. Same thing."

Brittany tilted her head, her expression sym-pathetic. "Well, since you'll be tutoring Holt's son, it sounds like you agreed to spend some se-rious time with the Dalton duo. And that means you might not have any say over what your heart says and does."

She'd become an expert at just that these past couple of years. A handsome face and a list of quali-ties she'd like hadn't been able to tempt her into dating anyone. "I pride myself on being levelheaded. Even if I'm attracted to Holt, I won't get involved with him. Tutoring his son will be about Robby. Not about me and Holt. There is no me and Holt."

"I do hear you, Amanda. But I'll say this. I'm glad you're going to tutor his son. Because you're putting yourself in the path. And that's where you should be, sweetie. Not hiding out in your room with Poindexter. Much as I love that cat."

Amanda wanted to tell her roommate—whom she adored—the same thing back. Brittany dated up a storm, but she never let anything escalate because she didn't want more than a good time. But what if her roommate did want more deep down where she wouldn't admit it to herself? Amanda had always figured the right guy would come along and Brittany's own words would be used against her. She'd be in the path and wouldn't be able to get out of the way.

Eh, life and love and relationships were complicated.

Brittany let out a giant yawn. "I'm zonked. And I can't wait to get out of this jumpsuit and into my pj's."

"The party was a huge success, I'm sure."

Brittany grinned and stood up. "It definitely was." She gave Poindexter a pat. "See you in the morning, roomie."

"Night, Brittany. Thanks for the talk."

With Poindexter in her arms, Amanda went into her bedroom. She got under the covers and knew she wouldn't be falling asleep any time soon. She stared up at the ceiling, trying to bore herself to sleep. But all she saw in her mind was Holt Dalton's face. And how sexy he was. She sighed and grabbed her phone, opening up her photos app.

Photos of Holt and Robby and their new dog and cat filled the screen. The craziest thought hit her and she quickly turned off her phone. She'd imagined herself in that last photo, sitting with Holt, her husband, Robby, her son, Bentley and Oliver—and of course Poindexter—her sweet pets.

She was getting all mixed up. She wanted a child—and obviously, Robby, with his put-it-out-there honesty and adorableness, had plucked her heartstrings something fierce. Throw in his gorgeous single father with whom she had a past, and of course her emotions were all over the place.

She took one last look at a photo of Holt before shutting off her phone and staring back up the ceiling. But all she saw was Holt's face. All she felt was Holt kissing her, his hands on her back. He was so familiar and so not at the same time.

How exactly was she going to keep herself from falling for him all over again?

* * *

Thunk.

Thunk-thunk.

Thunkety-thunk.

It was just before midnight. Holt glanced toward his bedroom door, not that it would reveal anything about the strange noises coming from down the hall. Sounded like Robby was bouncing one of Bentley's balls, but his son was fast asleep. He knew that because he'd come upstairs just a few minutes ago, checked on Robby, nodded at Bentley, who was lying at the foot of the bed, then went into his own room and slid under the covers, hoping he'd get some sleep tonight.

But doubting it. He could not stop thinking about Amanda and that kiss. Wanting more. Despite agreeing there would not be a second kiss.

Thunk.

Holt got out of bed and went to investigate.

"Daddy?" came Robby's voice.

"Already on my way," he called out, going into Robby's room.

Bentley was sitting on the floor by the bed now. Oliver was on his perch and jumped onto the foot of the bed, and the dog jumped up onto the bed too. Then the cat jumped down and Bentley did too.

Hence the thunks. Great—pet acrobatics at midnight.

"Bentley and Oliver," Holt said, wagging a finger. "You woke up Robby. Shhhhh from now on."

Bentley tilted his black-and-white head as if apologizing and agreeing. Oliver began grooming his face with a white paw. *Sorry, not sorry*, the cat seemed to be saying.

"I think I'll give Oliver a little more dinner right now," Holt said. He'd gotten that tip from Daphne. If he made the cat's dinnertime later, he'd likely sleep through the night. "Then he'll have a nice full belly and curl up to bed."

"'Kay, Daddy," Robby said with a yawn. He frowned, his face suddenly crumpling. "Daddy?"

Holt froze and then sat down on Robby's bed. "What's wrong, buddy?" He pushed his son's mop of brown bangs out of the way. Bentley jumped up and lay beside Robby to make sure his person was okay, and the boy put an arm around the sweet pooch.

"Do you think Gramps is still mad at me?" Robby asked.

Oh hell. A burst of anger radiated in Holt's gut. This was what Neal Dalton wanted? To worry a little kid so much that the first thing he thought of when he woke up in the middle of the night was that his grandfather was mad at him?

"Gramps loves you. I know that like I know my name. And yours. I promise you he does."

Robby shook his head. "But I'm loud and I break things."

"Gramps is just an impatient person. Something happens and he doesn't react well. Some people get mad if milk gets spilled or something breaks. Others, like Gram, take it a little easier. But Gramps loves you very much."

"Are you sure, Daddy?" his son asked, his expression less troubled.

"Yes. I'm sure." He *was* sure. His dad loved Robby like crazy; he had from the moment Robby was born. "Did I ever tell you what Gramps did right after coming to visit you in the hospital when you were just five minutes old?"

Robby giggled. "One million times, Daddy."

Okay, that was true. Holt pulled that one out of the hat so often because the story reminded him that his father *did* love the boy at the core, and it reminded Robby too in a way that seemed to settle inside his bones and cells, making him feel better.

"Well, I'm gonna tell you for the millionth and one time," Holt said, stretching out beside Robby and pulling his son against him. Bentley put his chin on Robby's belly with a sigh. "First your granddad stopped in the hospital gift shop, buying every single stuffed animal and like twenty 'It's A Boy!' balloons. Then he met you and held you for a long time, telling you how you were named after his favorite uncle who wasn't with us anymore. And when he bought Dalton's Grange, he planted an apple tree in the backyard that he named The Great Robby Dalton's Apple Tree."

Robby smiled. "I like my tree, Daddy. It gets bigger every year just like me."

"That's right. Your grandfather planted that in your honor, something superspecial that would last forever, right by the house."

"Gramps said he thought the tree would make apples in a few years," Robby said, letting out a giant yawn.

Holt nodded. "I'm already looking forward to the apple crumble you'll make me."

"I can't cook!" Robby said, laughing. But then he turned serious again. "Daddy, do you think my second grade teacher will like me?"

"Of course she will." The good news was that Robby had been assigned to Ms. Chang's classroom, and she had a reputation for being very patient and warm. "Warm and fuzzy" was good for Robby.

"Even though I'm in the worst reading group? I felt dumb when I was reading to Bentley and

Oliver. Do they think I'm dumb?" Tears filled his blue eyes again.

Oh no. "Robby," Holt said, drawing his son into his arms. "You are not dumb. You're very smart and you work very hard. Everyone learns to read at their own pace. Took me till the middle of second grade before I was considered a good reader. Just took me longer. Some things come easily and some things come harder. You can put together puzzles and Legos and figure out those crazy instructions. A lot of people can't."

"I am good at puzzles and Legos." His face brightened.

"Hey, did you know that Amanda works with kids at your school on reading and helping them improve? How would you like her to work with you the rest of the summer?"

In one day he'd gone from not having seen Amanda Jenkins for ten years to making an important decision—adopting Bentley and Oliver—in her presence and spending most of the evening with her. She'd met his parents—his entire family, actually. Then there was that amazing kiss. And now she'd be working with his son, probably a couple times a week for the rest of August. And August had barely begun.

Robby's face burst into a grin. "I'll be moved up from the worst reading group for sure!"

"I'll bet she can start working with you very soon." Holt liked the idea of having a very good reason to call Amanda in the morning. "You're a great kid. All you have to be is you, Robby. I love you just as you are. And so do Bentley and Oliver."

"Amanda likes me too," Robby said.

"She sure does."

Robby smiled, his entire countenance relaxing. "Good, Daddy."

"You feel better about everything?"

Robby nodded and yawned. "I'm so tired." He turned over and clutched his stuffed rodeo bull under his arm.

"I'm gonna go give Oliver that extra helping of food to calm him down. I think the thumps will stop and you'll be able to sleep."

"'Kay, Daddy. Love you."

Holt's heart was about to burst. "I love you too, Robby. Night."

"Night, Daddy," Robby said, his eyes closing.

Holt picked up Oliver, who wasn't having it and wiggled to be let down. "Fine, mister. You can follow me to the kitchen instead of having a perfectly good ride."

Which the cat did. As Holt put a little more dry food in the cat's bowl, Oliver padded over and began eating. *Ah, success*, he thought. *With a fully belly he'll settle down. No more thunks, for sure.*

As he put the bag of food away, he mentally added two items to his to-do list for the morning. One was to talk to his dad about how he was affecting Robby with his gruffness. The other was to ask Amanda to start working with Robby ASAP. Maybe even tomorrow.

Interesting that the thought of talking to Amanda made knowing he was going to have it out with his dad a lot easier.

Chapter Six

"I wish I had long nice hair like you."

Amanda glanced toward the voice. A little red-haired girl, three or four years old, with a chin-length bob, was staring at her from her seat at the big table in Tender Years Daycare, surrounded by kids practicing writing lower-case letters on wide-lined paper. Amanda was standing by the rows of cubbies, full of hoodies and lunchboxes, waiting for the daycare owner for their 10:00 a.m. marketing meeting.

"I love your hair," Amanda said.

The girl's face brightened. "Really? Mine was

long like yours but my little sister put gum in it
and my mommy had to cut it."

Aww. "Really and truly. And sorry about the
gum. That happened to me once. I'll bet by the
holidays your hair will be much longer."

"Really?" the girl asked. "By Christmas?"

Amanda did the math in her head. It was now
early August. The girl had a good five months to
go, and at half an inch a month, her hair would
be down to her shoulders by Christmas for sure.
"Yup."

"Yay," the adorable redhead said, and finished
coloring her picture of a cat.

Lucinda Banks, the owner of the daycare, gestured for Amanda to come back to her office. As
she walked past the precious bunch of children
working on their names, she took in their little
faces, so full of concentration and wonder, their
brightly colored sneakers and T-shirts, and her
heart almost burst.

As she followed Lucinda to her office, she was
grateful for the meeting this morning. Otherwise,
she'd be working at home as usual and would
be taking too many thinking-about-Holt breaks.
She'd woken up with him on her mind. She'd had
a quick breakfast in the kitchen with Brittany,
who'd told her to keep an open mind about the
sexy rancher. But she didn't want to. When you

had your heart broken into pieces by someone, how you could trust them again? How could you let yourself be that vulnerable? Amanda had finished her coffee and made a firm decision to close her mind concerning Holt Dalton.

Inside Lucinda's office, one wall devoted to children's artwork, Amanda spent the next forty-five minutes sharing her PowerPoint presentation. Lucinda approved her campaign ideas for both radio and local newspaper advertising and social media outreach to target ideal customers. Amanda had one more meeting with Bronco Bank and Trust and then a few hours of work to do at home. Finally she'd drive over to Dalton's Grange for her first tutoring session with Robby.

When she got home, she'd spend some solid time going over materials she had from the school district and some online sites for approaches to help struggling readers. She already had a good background, but with some focused prep for Robby's particular needs—luckily she'd already gotten a sense of that when he'd read to Bentley and Oliver yesterday—she'd feel even more armored to get Robby Dalton out of that "worst group."

She was all too aware that she was looking forward to that part of her day the most. To help Robby—and to see Holt again. The man she not an hour ago had firmly decided to keep at double arm's length. Somehow, she would.

As she was heading out of Lucinda's office, she noticed the group of preschoolers were now in circle time around a big colorful rug in the center of the room. Amanda paused by the front door as the teacher addressed the group.

"Boys and girls, in a little while we'll be drawing pictures of something that makes us feel happy," the teacher said. "Let's go around the circle and say one thing that makes you feel happy. Everyone will have a turn."

Being with Holt and Robby, Amanda thought unbidden—and was unnerved by her immediate response.

The teacher held up a yellow happy face on a stick. "I'll go first. My students make me happy—all of *you*!" She smiled and passed the stick to a student with a long brown braid who said that chocolate chip cookies for dessert made her feel happy. The girl then passed the happy face to the boy next to her.

"Recess time!" the boy with curly blond hair said.

"When my aunt Maya visits cuz she always brings me a present and she's coming today!" the next girl said.

"Coloring."

"Chicken nuggets but no yucky sauce."

"When my mommy picks me up from here and we go home."

Aww. Amanda felt her heart grow bigger and bigger as each little kid squeezed inside it. Now it was the redhead's turn, the one whose little sister put gum in her hair.

The girl tilted her head and thought for a second. "My little sister makes me happy because she's my little sister."

Double triple awww. I want a child, she thought. *I want to be a mother.* Maybe she should look into adoption—an older child. But as she pictured a little hand in hers, there was a man beside her holding the child's other little hand.

This wasn't matching up with Amanda's plans to avoid love and romance. And now because of the call she'd gotten just five minutes ago from Holt as she'd pulled into the parking area of the daycare, she'd be seeing Holt and Robby later—and likely twice a week for the next three weeks while she worked with the little Dalton on reading. Holt's description of Robby's worried wake up in the middle of the night had had her agreeing to help ASAP, which meant starting today. She and Holt had discussed setting up a regular schedule then too.

A regular schedule of being in Holt's house. With him there.

Suddenly, the little hand she imagined in hers was Robby Dalton's. The man beside her holding the other little hand: Holt Dalton. Oh boy. She could clearly see their faces now. Robby with Bentley on a leash beside him, Oliver hitching a ride on Bentley's back, which made no sense, but neither did thinking of Robby as hers in the first place. And on the other side of the boy was Holt, tall, sexy, strong Holt.

She was falling for him all over again. And she was in even bigger trouble this time around because his seven-year-old son had managed to steal her heart in record time. Her roommate's words came back to her yet again, about having an open mind. Could she? Despite everything that had happened? Everything she knew would happen?

And she did know. Holt would break her heart—again. Never in a million years would she have thought that summer ten years ago that Holt would have left her, dumped her flat on her face, without a backward glance. How did a person go from acting like he was in love, showing that love, to just walking away and cutting all ties?

Tyler had done the same thing.

So how could Amanda think of giving Holt a second chance? *Come on. You can't be your own worst enemy in life, girl*, she told herself. *Be your own best friend. Be your own Brittany! Do not let that man past Go. Or even close to Go.*

Then again, Holt hadn't exactly said anything about a second chance. In fact, when she'd broken up that amazing kissing session on his deck, he'd said he shouldn't be getting involved with anyone either, that he had a lot on his plate.

He *told* you this time. Said straight out that he wasn't looking for a relationship. And what had been her grandpop's motto? *When someone tells you who they are, believe them.*

If she let herself fall head over heels in love with Holt Dalton again, she'd only have herself to blame, not Holt, who'd been honest.

So. Do. Not. Let. Him. Pass. Go.

With that firm in her head, Amanda pushed open the door to leave Tender Years just as someone pulled it open to enter. She almost crashed right into none other than Neal Dalton, Holt's dad. He wore a dark brown Stetson, a western shirt under a jacket and jeans.

What on earth could he be doing here?

"Mr. Dalton," she said. "How nice to see you again. It was so thoughtful of your wife to invite me to the house for dinner last night."

He tilted his head at her, as if trying to remember her name. "Ah yes, Amanda, Holt's friend—

from way back at that summer camp he had to attend."

Had to attend. Where had Neal Dalton been ten years ago when that one little word would have clued her in that Holt wasn't telling her everything? She couldn't help but think if he had told her everything, he wouldn't have felt the need to break up with her. He'd have known that she wouldn't have judged him—especially not after getting to know him and loving him. But of course, that wasn't what happened.

"Call me Neal," he said with nod. "Sorry you saw me get so upset during dessert at Holt's. But that's exactly why I'm here. Do you work at the daycare?"

Uh, *why* was he here?

"No, I do marketing outreach and social media for Tender Years. I just had a meeting with Lucinda, the owner. But, Neal," she dared to press, "what do you mean that's why you're here?" Perhaps he wanted to volunteer at the daycare to learn more about how kids operated, that they made mistakes, they made noise, and to watch the teachers for tips on how to handle issues that arise.

"I want to find out if there's an opening for Robby for the rest of the month so that Holt can concentrate on the ranch," Neal explained. "With the day camp not willing to take him anymore, Holt's out of options. He already went through about five sitters who all quit and said Robby was just too much."

Amanda frowned. Granted, she hadn't spent *a ton* of time with Robby, but certainly enough to know the boy was just very energetic and curious and easily distracted. Robby had a good heart and understood right and wrong. He just needed to be around adults who knew how to channel that energy and curiosity. Tender Years was an excellent daycare with warm and experienced teachers; Robby would fit in well here from what Amanda had seen over the past year. "I didn't realize Holt was looking for a slot here for Robby. I can introduce you to Lucinda—"

"Oh, I haven't talked to Holt yet," Neal said. "I figured I'd find out if there was an opening and offer to pay the monthly cost to sway Holt to enroll Robby."

Amanda was sure her face registered her surprise—and alarm. "You mean you're here because *you* want Robby in daycare?"

"That's right. Full time till school starts up at the end of the month. Robby's a great kid, but he needs more structured activity and direction. Right now, with camps no longer an option, Deborah is watching Robby while Holt works, and granted, his uncles also help out, but wouldn't the boy be happier with scheduled activities and kids his own age? I thought I'd just see if there's an opening and then talk to Holt about it."

Amanda doubted Holt would want to put his son in daycare. She knew how much he valued the boy being around family for the rest of the summer.

"Anyway," Neal continued. "As I said, I'm just seeing if there's an opening. No harm in that."

But there was. And would be.

"May I help you, sir?"

Amanda turned and there was Lucinda, extending her hand toward Neal.

"Ah, Mr. Dalton, right? I believe I met you and your wife at a fund-raising dinner for the ranchers' association a couple months ago. You own Dalton's Grange, right? What a grand and gorgeous property. And you have all those handsome sons."

Neal took off his Stetson and shook her hand. "That's right. And a very energetic grandson who could use a place here, if there's an opening."

"I have an opening for a full-time or two part-time attendees," Lucinda said. "Come to my office and we'll discuss."

Neal put his hat back on, then tipped it at Amanda. "Nice seeing you again."

Amanda managed a smile and swallowed.
This was not going to end well.

Holt spent most of the morning herding cattle—
one of his favorite jobs on the ranch—into a farther
pasture, then helped his brother Morgan go over
inventory, and now, fortified by two strong cups
of coffee, it was time to find his dad and have that
talk. He'd been looking for Neal Dalton all morning but hadn't seen him anywhere. He tried the
main barn again, and there his dad was with his
usual clipboard, flipping pages of his to-do list
in one hand, his travel mug of coffee in the other.

Holt took a deep breath and cleared his throat.
"Glad I found you, Dad. I've been looking for
you all morning."

Neal took a long sip of his coffee. "Well, you
found me." He looked up at Holt as if bracing
himself. His dad clearly knew Holt wouldn't let
go of what happened last night with Robby.

But before Holt could launch into the sort of
speech he'd prepared in his head but had already
gotten jumbled, his dad spoke.

"So is this Amanda your girlfriend?" Neal
asked.

I wish, Holt thought, the words coming quicker
than he could deny them to himself.

Luckily, Holt didn't have to respond because

his father quickly added, "I ran into her this morning. I was walking in, she was walking out. Small world."

He ran into Amanda? "Walking out of where?" he asked, figuring his dad was at the coffee shop.

"Tender Years Daycare," Neal said. "She does marketing work for the place."

Holt stared at his father, feeling his eyes narrow. "Why were *you* there?"

Neal took another swig of coffee. "Well, that's what I wanted to talk to you about. Turns out the daycare has a full-time slot open. Robby could start tomorrow and stay until school starts. The boy could use some structure the next few weeks."

Whoa. Overstepping much? "Between his grandmother and his uncles, he has plenty of structure. His relatives enjoy spending time with him." He emphasized the word *relatives*, feeling his eyes narrow on his father even more.

Neal Dalton lifted his chin. "I know they do. I do too. I love Robby, Holt. But he's a whirlwind. Just think about the idea of the daycare—that's all I'm asking."

"I won't think about it," Holt said. "I have a good arrangement the next few weeks with Mom and my brothers watching Robby when I can't. We all planned it that way together, so they'd get to spend some real time with him this summer. I can hire a sitter now and again."

"The last few refused to come back," Neal reminded him.

"So I'll find someone else. I'm going to do what feels right to me, Dad. End of story."

"You were always unnecessarily stubborn," Neal said. "Amazing that that lovely young woman still likes you from when you knew her ten years ago." He tried to add a smile to show he was kidding, but Holt knew his dad wasn't joking in the slightest.

Holt crossed his arms over his chest. "Why wouldn't she?"

"Come on, Holt. Getting into trouble. Arrested twice for stupid stuff you shouldn't have been doing."

"That was a long time ago," he said, turning away.

"Look, Holt, I don't want trouble between us. That's the last thing I want. It means the world to me that you're here at Dalton's Grange with Robby. You know that. I'm just saying that my grandson—and I love that boy like mad—is a lot like you were at his age. Rein in him now and save yourself problems down the road."

A hot flash of anger burned red in Holt's gut.

"Oh, so now Robby's a juvenile delinquent in the making?"

"He needs structure, Holt. Plain and simple. More than baking cookies with Gram or mucking out the calf stalls for twenty minutes with your uncles."

"I think I know what my son needs, Dad."

"Why don't you ask that nice Amanda her opinion," Neal said. "She knows you from back when you used to be a troublemaker headed down the wrong path. That's why she's so understanding about Robby. She clearly sees you in him." Neal Dalton nodded as if doubly agreeing with himself, flipped through his clipboard a couple times, then glanced at Holt. "She'll tell you structure is a good thing for a rowdy child. I was too lenient with you and I regret it. That's what this is all about."

Holt felt like a character from the animated TV show his son loved, about a bull with a temper who always had locomotive steam coming out of his ears.

"What Robby needs," Holt said through gritted teeth, "is love and guidance and supportive people around him. You are *way* too hard on him. He's seven years old. He's a good kid, but yes, he makes mistakes. Yes, he talks too much and too loud, he runs when he should walk, he's impulsive. But the way you bark at him doesn't change his behavior."

Neal frowned. "I don't mean to bark. But sometimes I can't help it."

"Well guess what? Neither can Robby. He needs to be around his family right now—that's what I believe. I like the arrangement as it is, with me, his mom and his uncles watching him the rest of the month. I'm *not* sending him to Tender Years, wonderful as the place may be. End of discussion."

Holt was more than done with this conversation.

"Hey, Neal," a deep voice said from outside. "Got a sec to talk about where you want the shipment of hay bales coming in at noon?"

Holt glanced out the barn doors. Brody Colter, one of the ranch hands, was standing there, looking at Neal expectantly.

"Sure thing," Neal said to the guy. "Stubborn," he tossed at Holt, shaking his head as he walked out with his clipboard and his thermos.

Like father, like son, he wanted to call after him.

Chapter Seven

At a few minutes before five o'clock, Amanda pulled up in the drive at Holt's beautiful cabin. She could see Robby throwing a ball in a large fenced pasture at the side of the house, Bentley racing to get it, his furry tail wagging in the breeze.

Holt threw another ball to Robby, who couldn't catch it, but the smiling boy didn't seem to mind one bit. He ran after the orange ball, Bentley trying to get it first, and Robby was laughing so hard he dropped to his knees.

"You're faster than me, Bentley!" Robby said, giving the dog a rubdown. "I love you so much!"

Bentley put a paw on Robby's leg, and the boy was up like a shot, throwing the ball, which the dog went chasing after.

"Wow," Amanda said as she approached the fence, her tote bag with her reading supplies on her shoulder. "I knew Bentley was going to a great home, but to see him running around with a happy little boy, chasing balls, well, it warms my heart."

Holt nodded. "And they'll both sleep very well tonight. Not sure about me, though." His face hardened and he shook his head. "Heard you ran into my dad at a daycare in town."

Phew, she thought. On the drive over here, she'd hoped his father had already talked to Holt about that. Because if Neal hadn't, being here and having all that in her head with Holt none the wiser would have made her feel awful.

"Yeah," she said, wincing. "I asked why he was there and he told me. I had a feeling the conversation between you two would not go well."

"It didn't."

"How many hours does your mom watch Robby?"

"Two. Three to five, Monday through Friday. Just for August. Maybe he's too much on her, even though she's never said anything. I can hire a sitter so that there's more back up. Someone with really good references in handling high-energy kids."

Amanda bit her lip, working over an idea in her mind. A good idea? Bad idea? You-are-crazy-Amanda idea? She looked at Robby, throwing the ball for Bentley, then trying to race the dog to get it, his laughter a beautiful sound.

"I'm your gal," she said with a nod, then felt her cheeks burn. "I mean, I'll take over that time slot if it turns out your mom does need a break. Robby and I can spend an hour on reading and then an hour on playing with Bentley and Oliver. I can give him some really good training tips."

Holt stared at her, his expression a combination of wonder and surprise. "You'd do that? I'd pay you an amazing rate."

"Nope," she said. "I won't take a penny for helping Robby with reading, and I won't take a penny for hanging out with him. It's just three weeks. And to be honest, Holt, I want the experience."

He raised an eyebrow. "You have plenty of that, though. I'd pay any rate you asked."

She shook her head. "I don't mean experience tutoring. That I've got." She looked away, suddenly not wanting to say it—the reason.

He tilted his head and looked at her. Waiting.

She sucked in a breath. "Well, I've come to a

realization. I want a child. Since that likely won't happen the traditional way, I've been starting to think about adopting as a single mother. I just know I want to be a mother more than anything. And spending some real time with Robby, not in a classroom setting like at school, a couple hours every day will really help me figure things out. Maybe I am meant to adopt an older child."

Holt was still staring at her, not saying anything, and she could see he had questions that he hadn't really formed yet. *Same here, guy.*

"What do you mean that it won't happen the traditional way?" he asked. "Why not?"

"I told you—I gave up on love and thinking my Mr. Right, the man I'm meant to spend my life with, will come along. I like the idea of adopting an older child who needs a family."

Still the dark brown eyes were on her intently. He was taking it all in, she realized. Processing.

"You gave up on love because of me," he finally said, grimacing, his head dropping. "I'm so damned sorry, Amanda. If I could—"

She shook her head. "I kept my more recent past to myself. Two years ago I was engaged to be married and my fiancé left me at the altar. Almost literally. We were in Las Vegas, minutes from our appointment at the wedding chapel."

He sucked in a breath. "I'm very sorry."

She shrugged. "Like I said, I'm done with love. Romantic love, I mean. But I do want a child. And you need a sitter and I'd like to do my own first-hand research of sorts by spending lots of time with a child."

He had that slightly confused look on his face again. The processing.

"Yay, Amanda's here!" Robby suddenly said, and she turned toward his voice. He was smiling and waving at her, then kneeled beside Bentley. "Bentley, guess what? Amanda's gonna teach me to read better."

Amanda managed a smile at Robby and waved. She wasn't sure she could bear to continue this conversation with Holt, so she was glad it had come to an end.

"Can we continue this conversation after the tutoring session?" he asked. "Or tonight, actually. I'd like to assure us some privacy away from big ears," he added, upping his chin at Robby.

"Okay," she said, answering before her brain had time to process the consequences. Privacy. The two of them, alone. At nighttime. Just what had she gotten herself into here?

He held her gaze and nodded, then turned toward his son. "Robby, collect the balls and drop them in the bucket by the gate," he called over to him. "Then we'll head in to wash up before you start reading time with Amanda."

"'Kay, Daddy!" Robby said. "Bentley, come help me. You get that ball and I'll get this one." He pointed to the orange ball, and what do you know, the dog picked it up with his mouth and looked at Robby for next steps. Robby gasped. "Daddy, he did what I told him!"

Holt flashed Robby a thumbs-up. "Like Bentley, like Robby?" he whispered to Amanda with a warm, hopeful smile.

Robby ran over to the bucket and dropped the ball and pointed to it, and the dog dropped the ball right inside. The boy covered Bentley with hugs and praise.

"I don't always make the right choices," Holt said to Amanda. "But this," he added, nodding his chin at his son coming out of the gate with Bentley. "I knocked it out of the park."

"You sure did," she agreed.

Did I make the right choice by suggesting this little arrangement? she wondered. One minute she was resolving to keep an emotional distance from Holt. Now she'd suggested learning about motherhood by spending a lot of quality time with his son.

Holt glanced over at the gate. "Robby, latch the gate—always, right?" he called.

"Oh, right, Daddy." The boy turned back and latched the gate, and they all headed into the cabin.

Holt told Robby to wash his hands, and the boy scampered off.

"He and Bentley really are so good together," Amanda said, needing to keep the subject light right now. "Talk about a bonded pair from the get-go."

Holt nodded, his dark eyes so focused on her that she had to look away. She was too aware of him. Tall and strong and masculine, Holt Dalton filled a room, and they were in the small front hall where his presence was overwhelming. In a good way. "So where do want to work with him?"

"Normally I'd suggest a kitchen table, but I think Robby and I should work in his room. I want him to be at ease, in his element when he reads. And have a dog and cat around for support."

Again the smile he sent her could warm the coldest heart. "Sounds good. I like how you really seem Robby-focused instead of just reading-focused. I have such a good feeling about this, Amanda. And if I haven't said how much I appreciate that you're here, working with him…"

"It's my pleasure. Really." And she meant it.

Robby returned from the bathroom. "I'm ready to get better at reading now." He held up his washed hands, which smelled faintly of green apples.

"Robby, while you and Amanda are reading together," Holt said, "I'm going to Grams and Gramp's house to talk to Gram for a bit. I'll be back very soon."

"'Kay, Daddy. Tell them Bentley and Oliver say hi."

"And what about you?" Holt asked with a smile.

"Of course me too, Daddy!" Robby said, rolling his eyes in an exaggerated way at Amanda.

She laughed. "Let's go read in your room. Bentley can come too."

"Later, guys," Holt said, and headed out the door.

Later, guys. Just like he was leaving for a while and coming back to the house they shared…as husband and wife.

I'm going bonkers, she thought, shaking the wayward thoughts out of her mind as Robby ran upstairs, Bentley on his heels. She'd told herself she could not be having these fantasies about Holt—similar to ones she'd had a long time ago when she really did believe they were headed for marriage and children and forever.

They hadn't been then, though. And she'd better remember that they weren't now either. Or she'd have her heart rehanded to her.

* * *

Holt walked the half mile to the main house, barely aware of the breeze he'd normally be grateful for on a warm August afternoon. Amanda had been left at the altar? Who the hell would walk away from—

He shook his head at himself. *You, idiot. That's who.* He'd been young and stupid ten years ago. *Two* years ago, if she'd been his, he would have picked her up in his arms and run carrying her to that chapel to say I do.

And now she was planning a life that didn't include a husband. Which meant he was out before he was entirely even sure he should be counted in.

He wanted something, though. A second chance. A shot. He'd loved Amanda fiercely ten years ago and she was that same beautiful person, inside and out—kind, compassionate, interesting, smart, funny. Except now, the girl who'd been so open was a guarded woman—for good reason.

He'd helped put up those walls and maybe he could try to take them down. If she let him anywhere near her heart again.

He did have the child she wanted and already seemed to adore, but Robby was a package deal with his dad. Holt frowned, kicking at a rock in his path. Usually Holt had to tell women that *he* was a package deal. Now, the woman he couldn't stop thinking about had no interest in getting involved with him.

Well, he certainly helped put that plan into motion for her ten years ago, and some jerk cemented it.

And that's it? he asked himself. *You're just gonna give up that easily? Show her who you are, that you've changed, that you wouldn't hurt her again, that you'd never walk away from her.*

He didn't know how to do that, though. It wasn't like she'd date him. She'd made that clear. He'd have to show her on the down-low, in the times they were together. Before and after the tutoring sessions. If Holt's mom *was* okay with her two hours a day of watching Robby on the weekdays, he could always suggest to Amanda that she simply come work with Robby every day on reading. That way, she'd still get a lot of time with him.

He reached the main house, struck as always by its grandeur. His father sure had hit the jackpot—literally. Holt wasn't a gambler, and poker and slot machines and the tables had ruined his father a time or two before, but he'd gotten very lucky and now he'd given his wife all this. His parents had gone from having barely anything to their name but a run-down small ranch to absolute wealth on anyone's terms. Holt tried to see the bright side of that, even if his mother would have been happy with a ranch a quarter of this size, this majestic. Deborah was about family, not money.

Which brought him back to why he'd come. He shook off his thoughts and entered the house, hearing the sound of talk radio coming from down the hall. He followed it to the "Mom-dom." That was his term for his mother's sanctuary, a large, sunlit room that was part home office, part library, part crafts room and *all* Deborah Dalton, down to the apricot-colored walls and watercolor paintings of the Montana wilderness. His mom sat at her desk and was on her computer, an invoice up on the screen, scrolling through an upcoming cattle auction.

"Hi there, Holt," Deborah said, smiling up at him. "Got my precious grandson with you?"

Now that was what he liked to hear. He certainly wasn't going to put his mother on the spot—or cause a problem between her and his father. He'd just feel things out and get a sense of how his mother felt. Deborah Dalton was a kind, loving person who tended to put others first. She'd never come out and say that Robby was too much for her, but Holt had always been able to read his mom well. He'd know.

"Actually, Robby's at the house with Amanda right now. She's tutoring him in reading starting today. She volunteers at the elementary school and has a lot of experience. And best of all, Robby really likes her."

"I can understand why. Amanda seems lovely. You really like her too?" his mother added with a sly smile.

"Actually yes," he admitted. "But I messed up ten years ago, and I doubt she'll give me another chance. She's already planning a future without me or even any husband in it."

His mother raised an eyebrow. "Really? What do you mean?"

He wasn't so sure he should be talking about Amanda's personal life this way, but he'd always been able to talk to his mom, and right now he needed some advice. "Between what I did ten years ago and getting left at the altar two year ago, she says she's done with love and romance. She wants a child, though, and is thinking about adopting an older kid. She even suggested working with Robby every day on his reading and then spending another hour just playing so she can get some 'mother experience.' In other words, in three weeks, when Robby goes back to school, I won't see her anymore."

"Well, I'll tell you, Holt. She may have given up on love—or think she has, anyway—but if you have feelings for her, then see what you can do about changing her mind. Minds can be changed. Trust me."

He glanced at his mom, wondering if she was referring to herself and the rough patches she'd had with his dad.

"I do, absolutely," he said.

She stood up and came around the desk and held out her arms. "You're never too old to hug your mama."

He smiled and let her wrap him in one of her big hugs, the kind Robby loved so much.

"Oh, you know, Holt, I wonder if Amanda's request to spend two hours a day with Robby might work out timewise. I signed up for an intensive knitting class that meets every weekday from three o'clock to five o'clock for the next two weeks. Usually I watch Robby at that time and figured I'd switch times with your brothers. But maybe Amanda can fill in?"

Could this have worked out any better? "She'd love to, so that's perfect. Listen, Mom, I want to ask you something and I want your complete honesty. Deal?" Now that she was off the hook, he felt comfortable coming right out with the question.

"Of course," she said, sitting back down.

"Is Robby too much?" he asked.

"For me? If you're asking if that's why I signed up for the knitting class, absolutely not. I adore my grandson and spending these two hours a day with him is a highlight, Holt. Yes, he's a whirlwind, but he's a sweetheart—and I'm not saying that because he's my grandson. Robby has a huge heart and means well. I love that boy to pieces, and there's no way I'm giving up my summertime with him. I'll split the difference with his uncles and get my Robby time that way."

He'd known before he walked in here that this was how his mother felt about his son, but hearing it filled him up.

"Dad thinks he's too much," he said quietly. He wanted his father to feel about Robby the way his mother did. Not want to get him out of his hair for the next three weeks.

"Your father thinks just about everything is too much," Deborah said, her blue eyes twinkling. "The price of feed. The news. The way Shep races his horse. The weather. I could go on." She shook her head with a smile.

"Thanks, Mom," he said, getting up, feeling like two heavy rocks had been lifted off his shoulders.

On the way home, it struck him that his mother's new knitting class sure seemed coincidental. Same time that she watched Robby? For the next two weeks? And it had come up just as he'd brought up Amanda being available? *Uh-huh. Sure, Mom.*

He had a feeling Deborah Dalton was playing matchmaker. And loved her even more for it.

Chapter Eight

When Holt came back to his house a half hour later, he could just make out Robby's voice upstairs. He heard laughter, a combination of his son's hearty laugh and Amanda's. Then he heard Robby say something and again more laughter. If the boy was having this much fun getting tutored in reading, Amanda deserved a million bucks and a gold medal. And his everlasting thanks.

And dinner, which he hoped she wouldn't find presumptuous. This morning, he'd promised Robby one of his favorites, chicken parm with spaghetti and garlic bread, and he did recall Amanda ordering a chicken parm sub from a pizza place on their trip into town on one of their days off from camp, so he knew she liked it. Maybe she'd say thanks but no thanks and leave. Or maybe she'd stay. He was hoping for *stay*. She'd been here for thirty minutes, which meant another thirty to go—exactly when dinner would be ready. No one could resist the smell of garlic bread, right?

By the time the cheese was melting and the garlic bread smelled so good that his stomach rumbled, he heard Robby running down the hall upstairs. "Daddy!" came his son's booming voice. "I smell something amazing! Amanda, doesn't that smell amazing?"

"Sure does," he heard her say.

Half a minute later, Robby was sniffing his way into the kitchen, Amanda right behind him.

"That really does smell intensely good," she said. "Garlic bread and what else?"

"Chicken parm!" Robby said, rubbing his hands together. "Daddy promised me he'd make it tonight."

"And I made enough for three," Holt said, catching Amanda's gaze. "Stay? We'd like to thank you for what definitely sounded like a good first day of reading practice."

"It was fun, Daddy," Robby said. "I read a

book—a chapter book!—to Amanda about a dog named Joey who has a cat for a best friend! Just like Bentley and Oliver. And Amanda said I can keep the book too. And yes, I said thank you."

Holt smiled. "Good. How about you go wash up for dinner and meet us in the dining room?"

Robby ran off, and Amanda moved closer into the kitchen, giving the air a sniff.

"I was just a little hungry before but now I'm starving," she said. "That just smells too good."

Thank you, universe, he sent heavenward. "Great."

She leaned against the counter, looking so sexy in her dark jeans and pale pink tank top, white stars embroidered on the V-neckline. Her hair was in a braid down one shoulder. She'd dressed casually, instead of more "teacher-like" to make Robby feel comfortable, he realized. "Talk go okay with your mom?"

He dragged his attention off how pretty she was and onto her question. "Better than okay. And you're on for the every weekday arrangement. Turns out my mom is taking an intensive knitting class that meets every day at that time for the next two weeks, so I'd need someone to fill in for her anyway. She wants to keep watching Robby, so she'll switch some morning hours with one of my brothers."

Her eyes widened as if she hadn't fully expected it to work out. "I'm glad. Wow, I'll really get to put my plan into motion—to get a sense of what it would be like to be a mom of a child Robby's age. I mean, not that spending two hours a day with him is anything close to what goes into raising a child, but I'll get a real sense, you know?"

"I think it's great that you want to be a mom and that you're thinking of an older child. That's beautiful, Amanda. There are a lot of kids out there who need loving homes." *There's also an open slot in my own small family for someone who loves kids and dogs and cats*, he thought.

Whoa—that notion slammed into him with startling force. He'd gone from thinking about the possibility of a second chance to marriage? Holt wasn't used to being led around by his heart, not that he'd used his brains much when he was younger either. But these days, he was six feet two inches of emotion. And given that Amanda had told him a second chance was off the table, he'd better be careful with himself.

But now Amanda was smiling so warmly at him that he wanted to gather her into his arms and just hold her and never let her go.

Luckily, Robby was back and dinner was ready, so he focused on plating everything. Robby

carried the platter of garlic bread with two hands
into the dining room, while Amanda brought in
the salad and he carried the platter of chicken
parm. They sat at the big table, big enough for
his whole family and a guest or two, but because
they were all at one end, it felt cozy. And right.
Him. Robby. And Amanda.

Every time he looked at that chair, he'd be reminded of that open slot.

For his wife. For a mother for Robby.

Robby pronounced the chicken parm "too good
for words," and Amanda seconded that. They ate
and drank iced tea and talked about Robby's reading practice, and how patient Bentley was to sit
through three books over the hour. They talked
about their favorite seasons and foods and TV
shows, and suddenly it was as if ten years hadn't
gone by, and he and Amanda were those same
two kids, lying on the grass by lake and holding
hands, talking about everything. He could barely
take his eyes off her during dinner. *I am you and
you are me...*

With mere crumbs left on everyone's plate,
Amanda insisted on helping him clear the table.
In the kitchen, while he scooped out the ice cream
for their dessert, he asked if she was okay staying
a bit later after Robby went to bed so they could
work up the schedule—and talk more about her

idea to adopt. And why. Holt had said he wanted to continue that conversation, which had surprised her.

She hesitated for a moment, then said, "Sure. I can stay for a bit."

He smiled to himself, well aware that she was a little nervous about being alone with him, about their undeniable attraction, about whether despite what they'd agreed to, they'd end up kissing again.

Maybe they'd end up in bed, where Holt would love to spend some time with Amanda Jenkins.

He knew that was a pipe dream given all she'd said earlier, but he was still filled with anticipation about later. About possibilities. Maybe they *could* have a second chance. Maybe he *could* change her mind, let her see that he was someone she could trust.

Twenty minutes later, ice cream sundaes consumed, Amanda insisted on cleaning up since Holt had cooked, so Holt and Robby went into the yard with Bentley. Robby asked Amanda if she'd watch his favorite before-bed TV show with him, about the bull, so the three watched that together, Amanda on the big club chair perpendicular to the sofa, him and Robby on the couch. Through the show, Holt kept picturing the three of them sitting on the sofa—Robby between them—every night after dinner. Right now she was keeping a bit of a distance, which he totally understood.

After Robby's quick bath and a story and his good-night routine with Bentley and Oliver, which included having Robby say good-night to each from each, the boy was asleep in his bed, his arm wrapped around his stuffed rodeo bull. And he and Amanda finally were alone to talk.

He came downstairs to find her looking at the framed photographs on the fireplace mantel. There were a lot of pictures. Mostly of Robby, and a lot of the boy with his uncles and grandparents, plus a few from when Holt was a kid. He did have a photo of him and Amanda from ten years ago, which he kept in the drawer of his bedside table. Sometimes over the years he'd pull it out and wonder where she was, what she was doing.

Now she was right here.

"Robby did very well earlier," she said, turning around. "I think I can help him get moved up at least two levels by the time school starts."

"That's great, Amanda. Thank you. Really."

She sat back down in the club chair, avoiding being next to him on the sofa, unfortunately. "So the plan is that I'll come every day at three o'clock for reading time, then at four, we'll switch to playtime. I don't have to work with Robby on reading every day—maybe three times a week so that it doesn't feel like school. There are lots of ways to make reading feel joyful, but it's still hard work for him, so I need to be careful of not overdoing it."

"Sounds good. Scratch that—it sounds amazing. I don't know how I got so lucky, Amanda. The reading help from someone experienced and compassionate who really gets Robby. And the babysitting time. I know it helps you out too, but I really can't thank you enough."

"I'm really happy about the arrangement."

"I have no doubt you'll make an incredible mother, Amanda. You're loving and kind and Robby is nuts about you. He's a very good judge of character."

The big, happy smile on her beautiful face told him how much this plan of hers really meant to her. She might be at the starting gate with even thinking about motherhood, but being a mom was in her heart; he could clearly see that.

"I think about everything you're saying and how my son's own mother doesn't feel that way." He shook his head. "I hate that I had something to do with you giving up on love, though," he said with a grimace. "I know you got hurt again after our relationship, but I just wish I'd been different back then." He really needed to take a giant step back.

She looked at him for a moment, then said, "To the future, then. Everything is about what's ahead."

But here he was, focused on the past—and moving backward, not forward.

And now they were pretty much done with discussing the plan, but he wasn't ready for her to leave yet. Maybe there was more to say. "Coffee? We can clink to the new arrangement."

She smiled again. "Sure."

He got up to make it and brought it in the living room to find her once again looking through the photos on the mantel. As he set the tray of mugs and the sugar bowl and creamer on the coffee table, she sat down in front of it on the sofa. He sat beside her.

She added cream to her coffee. "I have a few pictures of you from that summer we were a couple. Sometimes I'd take one out and wonder where you were, what you were doing."

He turned and stared at her. "I did the same thing. And was just thinking about that when I came down and saw you looking at the family photos. When I got divorced I thought about looking you up, but—"

"But what?" she whispered.

It wasn't easy for him to think back to those days. "I guess I felt like I was in a bad place.

Newly divorced, a young son who didn't understand where his mother was."

She reached for his hand and gave it a gentle squeeze. He held on to her hand, looking into her eyes, leaning toward her a bit…leaning a bit more until their lips touched. She moved closer to him, his hands on either side of her face, then in her hair, across her back. He loved the feel of her, the lightly perfumed scent of her.

He couldn't get enough of Amanda, his hands now traveling up the back of her tank top, her soft bare skin driving him insane. He remembered the first time they made love, when they went camping on their day off, and he felt so much that he thought his heart might actually explode.

But now she was pulling away, fixing her tank top and smoothing her hair. "Holt, I can't. I said so. You said so. We can't do this."

"But if we both want to and clearly we do—"

She shook her head. "I'm attracted to you. No doubt. But like I said, I'm done with romance. And certainly with someone who broke my heart so bad I can still remember how hurt I was ten years later. I'm sorry, Holt. But I won't go there." She grabbed her bag and headed for the door. "I don't want to disappoint Robby, so I won't back out on him. But no more, Holt. We don't sit on the same sofa anymore. Got it?"

He managed something of a smile that he hardly felt. "Got it."

At least he knew for absolute sure that she was still attracted to him. The kiss last night could have been chalked up to nostalgia. But tonight had been pure chemistry and undeniable heat.

He just had to prove to her that he'd changed, that he was the guy she'd always thought he was. He had a solid two weeks to do that, while she was here every day.

And dammit, he'd do it.

"Good luck with that," Brittany said with a warm smile. She and Amanda sat at the kitchen table in their condo the next morning, Amanda on her second cup of coffee and a barely touched bagel after telling her roommate all that had happened yesterday. "Look, I get why you're wary of Holt. But like I said before, keep an open mind—even just a smidge open."

Amanda grimaced. "My mind *is* a smidge open—otherwise I wouldn't have kissed him back last night. My hands were all over his chest! That brought back some serious memories. For a second there, I was so lost in ten years ago that I forgot I'm supposed to sit far away from Holt whenever we're alone in a room together."

Brittany laughed, tucking an errant long ring-

let behind her ear. "Yeah, good luck with that
too. You like him too much. You have too much
history. And you're too attracted to him for that.
You know, Amanda, the read I'm getting based on
everything you said happened yesterday and the
day before is that Holt Dalton is still very much
in love with you."

A little burst of sadness made its way from her
stomach to her chest, stopping on the left side.
She shook her head. "How in love could he have
been, Brittany? He just walked away."

"Because he was going back to nothing, honey.
Back to the guy he was before he met you."

Huh. Amanda hadn't thought of it that way.
"Go on," she said. "I'm listening." Thank God
for insightful roommates.

Brittany took a sip of her coffee. "He was
headed down the wrong road in those days, right?
Getting into trouble with the law for minor of-
fenses. No plans for his life after dropping out of
college. No job, no direction. And didn't you say
he had some issues with his father? So he couldn't
just go home. He had nowhere to go and that's
where he thought he would take you, Amanda.
So he broke up with you instead."

Amanda gasped. "You're right. You are one
hundred percent right. That makes total sense to
me." She sat back, kind of stunned. She'd never

been able to understand how a guy who'd obviously loved her—and Holt had, she was sure of it—could have just dumped her that way, torn them apart and taken off as if the whole summer hadn't happened. Now she knew. He'd done it for *her*.

She stared at her sesame bagel, something poking at her heart. "But, Brittany, I could have helped turn his life around. He knew that too. I would have set him on the right path. He didn't trust in that. That says something too."

"Yeah, it says he didn't trust in love or people enough for that because of what he'd gone through in his own life. It's not about you, Amanda. I know it's hard not to take it personally. But his reasons and thought processes when he left you—it was about him."

"I hear you. I don't like it, but I hear you."

"I can be louder if you need it," Brittany said, grinning. "Any time you need some coaxing over to the love side, you just let me know."

"And what about you?" Amanda asked, raising an eyebrow.

"I date plenty. But I like my singlehood just the way it is."

Her roommate had met a lot of special someones. And she'd let them all go. When she was ready, she'd be ready. That was all there was to it.

Brittany had to get to work, so Amanda cleaned up, played with Poindexter for a few minutes and then sat down at her desk in her bedroom. She checked her email—for the millionth time—hoping there would be a response or two about her post on the chat group of people with adoption queries. She wanted to have good news for her friend and neighbor, Mel, about the whereabouts of Beatrix Abernathy—the long-lost baby that Mel's fiancé's great-grandfather had had to give up for adoption seventy-five years ago.

There *was* a response!

Dear Amanda, I hope you connect with the person you're looking for. I found a half sister I never knew existed through this group so don't give up hope if it takes a while to get a lead.

Amanda's heart sank that the response wasn't from someone who did have a lead on Beatrix, but at least some kind person out there was sending good wishes her way, particularly someone who had connected with the person she'd been looking for. Amanda did appreciate that. Especially because she had no idea how they'd ever find Beatrix otherwise with such little information to go on.

Someday I will find a way to bring her back to you...

Josiah Abernathy's words to his young love, Winona Cobbs, filled her mind, all the determination in that letter he'd tucked inside his journal, buried under the floorboards of his old ranch house for seventy-plus years.

Where are you, Beatrix Abernathy? she wondered. Right here in Bronco? For all Amanda knew, she'd walked past her in town countless times over the past two years. *I sure hope we find you.*

There were so many ways people, loved ones, got separated from one another.

You and Holt have a second chance. Stop resisting it, a little voice said.

Oh, you resist it, Amanda Jenkins, and hard! another, louder little voice said. *That man will crush your heart again. Mark my words. It was all about him then and it is now.*

Poindexter jumped up on her desk and sat right beside her laptop.

"What to do, Poin?" she asked the wise cat. "Give me a sign."

Poindexter began grooming his face with his paw, which told her nothing. Except that maybe she should start researching adoption instead of just thinking about it. She typed Wyoming Department of Family Services into the search engine and clicked on Foster Care and Adoption Requirements. She could foster a child or adopt as a single person—that was good. She read about how to become a foster parent, which seemed the way to begin the process since she wanted to adopt an older child. A half hour passed and she'd taken pages of notes, excited and a little scared at what a huge undertaking this would be.

She glanced at the time; she had to get into the shower and get cracking on her to-do list. She had a busy schedule of work at home and two meetings, and then she'd head back to Holt's house to work with Robby and spend time with her favorite seven-year-old.

She thought about Brittany's "good luck with that," which made her worry that this attraction thing with Holt was out of her hands, that she couldn't stop it or even try to. Amanda was pretty sure her roommate was right about that. Maybe all the reason to work harder at remembering how badly he'd hurt her, that it *had* been all about him so she wouldn't get her head all turned around.

She'd focus on Robby when she was at the Dalton home. Not his superhot dad.

Chapter Nine

"Guess what, Daddy?" Robby said when he and Amanda came in from the backyard. It was already five which meant Robby and Amanda's two hours together had come to an end. "I read a whole line today without having to stop. I didn't get messed up!"

Holt's heart moved in his chest and he smiled at his son. "I'm proud of you, Robby. You're working hard and it's already paying off."

Robby nodded. "Does that mean we can have pizza for dinner?"

Holt laughed. "I am dying for pizza, actually."

He turned to Amanda, once again hoping she'd say yes. "Join us? My treat."

"I'm getting pepperoni and mushroom, my favorite," Robby said. "What's your favorite pizza, Amanda?"

"My favorite is just plain cheese, actually. Just the crust, sauce and mozzarella cheese. Perfection. And now I can't stop thinking of having some pizza."

"Yay, Amanda's coming," Robby shouted, clapping his hands.

He smiled and glanced at Amanda. He had to give her an out to show her he had heard her last night and would respect how she felt about the two of them spending non-necessary time together. "Robby, Amanda might already have dinner plans."

She looked at him, then at Robby. "What? And miss pizza? No way. And besides, there's a great place not too far from my apartment building, so I'd be passing it anyway."

She'd definitely added that so he'd know this was strictly about convenience and a craving, but there was hope for a second chance here, he knew. And he was taking it.

Twenty minutes later they were inside Bronco Brick Oven Pizza, sitting at a round table and awaiting their orders. For the first time in a long time, Holt was sitting with his son and a woman inside a restaurant, and he liked it. Usually it was just him and Robby, all the time, everywhere they went. Yeah, his parents or brothers joined them sometimes, but there always seemed to be an absence. He knew that Robby wasn't aware of it most of the time; he knew his son very well—and he could always tell when Robby *was* aware of it. He certainly wasn't now. His adorable face was free of any kind of sadness. Robby had clearly had a good time with Amanda earlier, and was equally happy that she was with them now.

Just after the waiter set down their drinks, a cute kid about Robby's age with red hair and freckles came up to their table. A woman who looked a lot like him and a little girl were behind him.

"Hi, Robby!" the boy said.

Robby grinned. "Hi, Liam. The pizza here is soooo good, right?"

"I had like a million slices," Liam said with a big nod. "We just signed up for the fun run," he added, pointing to a poster and sign-up sheet on the far wall. "I want to win this year. Last year I was one of the last kids."

Holt smiled. "Well, it's a fun run so it's all about fun. Good for you for entering!" He smiled up at the mom, then turned to his son. "Robby, would you like to sign up?"

Robby nodded with a grin. "I love running and I'm good at it."

"The fun run really is fun," the woman said. "It's a mother-son event that the pizzeria is sponsoring."

Holt's stomach twisted at the words *mother-son*. He watched Robby's face fall as he stared down at his cup of soda.

"I can barely run half a mile," the woman continued, oblivious, "but I actually pulled it off last year. And it was great to do something like that with my son. Are you a runner?" She directed the question to Amanda. "You and Robby should enter!"

"I'm kind of a couch potato," Amanda said, glancing at Holt to interject—and fast.

"Well, think about it," the woman said before he could say a word. "Nice seeing you," she added before heading toward the door.

"I wish I could do the fun run but I can't because my mom isn't around," Robby said, tears filling his eyes and streaking down his face.

Holt stood up and knelt beside Robby. "Hey, there," he said, pulling his son into a hug. Robby cried harder, burying his face in Holt's shirt.

Holt looked at Amanda, sure his own his expression mirrored the heartbreak on hers.

Suddenly, she pointed at herself and mouthed, *I could run with him.*

He was so moved he could barely process it. Holt pressed his hand to his chest and mouthed back *thank you.*

"You know, Robby," Amanda said, "I might be a couch potato—meaning I'm usually on my couch instead of outside jogging—but I'd love to do the fun run with you. If you want."

Robby's face emerged and he wiped under his eyes. "But it's a mom and son run."

"I'll bet if I read the rules on the poster," Amanda said, "they'll say that you can run the race with me. I'll bet tutors are allowed."

Robby brightened. "Really? Can we check?" He ran over to the poster on the opposite side of the pizzeria.

Again, Holt was so touched by what she'd said that he couldn't find his voice. As she stood to follow Robby, he reached for her hand to stall her. "You're the absolute best, Amanda Jenkins."

She smiled, holding his gaze for a heartbeat, then glanced at where Robby was standing. "It would be my pleasure. Really."

This was about more than wanting experience at motherhood. *This*, right now, was about how she felt about Robby, one particular seven-year-old who happened to be his beloved child. She cared about Robby very much. Did she know how much that meant to him?

Robby was waving her over. As Holt and Amanda headed to the poster, he sent up a silent prayer that the rules didn't actually say mothers and sons only. That would be nuts, right? Not every child had a mother. "Can you help me read the rules, Amanda?"

Holt smiled to himself at that.

Amanda scanned the fine print, which was minimal. "Hmm, this event is open to boys ages five to eleven and an adult female relative, caregiver, teacher, or family friend." She turned to Robby. "That's me. Family friend. So let's do this!"

"Yay!" Robby said, jumping and clapping.

The people at the table closest smiled in that "he's kind of loud" way. Holt ignored them but ushered Robby and Amanda back to their seats just as their pizzas were served.

"I can't believe I get to do the fun run!" Robby said, picking up his slice of pizza.

Amanda lifted her plain slice too. "Hope you don't mind that I'm not very fast."

"I'm really glad because I'm not fast either," Robby said, giggling.

From tears to giggles just like that.

For the third or fourth time since Amanda Jenkins came back into his life, Holt felt his heart move inside his chest.

Holt had just left Robby's room after reading him a story and telling him a story—about the tortoise and the hare, which he loved—when the knocking on the front door began. He glanced at his phone for the time. Past nine.

That was weird. Since arriving in town a year ago, Holt had kept to himself, well, except for the dating he'd done when he'd first moved here, trying to find his Ms. Right and a mother for Robby and failing miserably on both counts. He hadn't made friends off the ranch; he simply had no time between work and raising his son. His brothers were his social life. And none of them would be banging on the door this late, knowing it was past Robby's bedtime.

Maybe it was Amanda. Maybe she'd changed her mind about doing the race with Robby. About their entire arrangement. Holt sure hoped that wasn't the case.

But no way would Amanda be knocking on the door right now. She wouldn't risk waking up Robby either; she would have texted to say she was outside.

Holt glanced out the window on the second-floor landing. A silver Range Rover was idling in the drive. Did he know anyone who drove a Range Rover? He didn't think so.

Bentley had come bounding out of Robby's room and stood at the top of the stairs, waiting for him. Luckily, the dog didn't bark and wake up Robby, who'd finally gotten to sleep after being so excited about participating in the fun run with Amanda. They headed down, Holt wondering who was on the other side of the front door.

With Bentley at his side, Holt opened the door to find a total stranger with a spitting mad expression. Whoa, dude. The man was in his late forties, maybe early fifties, with a receding hairline and a bit of a paunch. He wore expensive leather shoes—not the work boots or cowboy boots you saw on a cattle ranch.

"You Holt Dalton?" the man asked, anger radiating out of his narrowed blue eyes.

"I am," he said. Once upon a time, Holt would have deflected, given his troublemaking days. Now, he had nothing to hide. "What's this about?"

"I went to the main house and spoke to the owner of the ranch. A Neal Dalton. He said to talk to you."

Huh? His dad had told this man to come talk to Holt? "About?" he asked, wondering what the hell was going on. He stepped out onto the porch, letting Bentley out too, and keeping the front door just slightly ajar.

"One of your cowboys, ranch hands, whatever the hell they're called, is corrupting my daughter," the man said. "She's only eighteen and a college freshman. I want you to call him off."

Holt gaped at the man. "Call him off? What's the issue, exactly?"

"The issue is that he's a troublemaker who is not going to mess up my daughter's life. I want you to put an end to their relationship."

So this man had gone to the main house, spit out this request, and Holt's dad had sent the guy here? Why?

Because Holt had once been that cowboy? And Amanda had been that corruptible daughter who had to be protected from the likes of him at all costs? He'd never met Amanda's dad, but if the man had known about Holt's past he probably would have tried to talk her away from him too.

"Who's the hand?" Holt asked.

The man seemed to relax, as if he thought he was finally getting somewhere, that Holt would take care of it. Holt had no clue what he'd do. But he wanted to know who he was dealing with. Dalton's Grange employed a slew of cowboys, some part-time, particularly in the spring and summer.

"His name's Brody Colter. He's a real punk."

Brody. Holt knew who he was. It had been Holt who Neal had sent to bail the guy out of jail about three months ago. Brody had been charged with assault in a bar fight but the charges had been dropped. Holt didn't know the ranch hand well, but according to Neal, Brody was one of their best cowboys—never late, good at his job, respectful of others. He'd been working at the ranch part-time during high school and since he'd graduated in June had gone full-time. Getting into a bar brawl and ending up in jail—no one to bail him out but his boss—didn't fit with Holt's image of Brody Colter at all.

"In what way?" Holt asked.

"First of all, he's been in trouble with the law. Second, he practically lives at Wild Wesley's, that dive bar out in Bronco Valley, and I've heard stories about that place. And third, my daughter just graduated from high school two months ago. She's headed to college at the end of the month. Suddenly, she's saying she thinks she met the love of her life and that maybe she could take a year off. That punk is not the love of her life, and she's not losing her scholarship to Wyoming Western College. Over my dead body!"

"Mr…" Holt prompted.

"Thompson. Edward Thompson. I'm the senior

VP of new development for Thompson Paper—
a business that's been in my family and Bronco
Heights for almost a hundred years. My daughter's name is Piper. Short for Pauline. Do I have
your word you'll take care of this problem?"

"Mr. Thompson, you said your daughter is
eighteen. So is Brody. I'm not sure how anyone
can prevent them from dating."

Thompson crossed his arms over his chest.
"Apparently Brody likes this job. Threaten him
with it. Tell him he either stops seeing Piper or
he's fired. If the job means that much to him, he'll
move on to another pretty girl—this time from
Bronco *Valley.*"

This time from Bronco Valley. Until they'd
moved to Bronco Heights from Whitehorn, the
Daltons had always been from the wrong side of
town. So Holt knew exactly what the man meant,
and he didn't like it. Or Edward Thompson. What
a pompous—

"I said what I came to say," Thompson huffed.
"I'm a big donator to the ranchers' association,
and I think the powers that be over there would
want to keep me in their good graces."

Now he was threatening Holt and Dalton's
Grange? Thompson wouldn't make a donation
unless Holt intervened, and if Holt didn't, the loss

of big bucks to the association would be the Daltons' fault?

I don't think so, buster.

The man was down the porch steps before Holt could respond and that was probably for the best. He got in his silver Range Rover and drove off.

Holt sat down on the porch swing, shaking his head. "Believe that guy, Bentley?"

The dog rested his chin on Holt's knee, and he rubbed the sweet pooch's furry head.

Brody didn't live on Dalton's Grange. There were two bunkhouses a mile out back on the property that some full-time hands shared, but Holt recalled that Brody had his own tiny apartment, an efficiency, right above Wild Wesley's. Man, that had to be loud all night long, particularly Thursday to Saturday nights. He knew this detail about where Brody lived because he'd dropped the guy off there after bailing him out of jail, and Holt had said, "You just got busted for getting into a fight here, now you're going back for more? I don't like wasting my money, Brody."

And Brody had again insisted he didn't start the fight nor had he wanted to participate in it, then explained he lived above Wild Wesley's, thanked Holt again for bailing him out, then had gone in a narrow door wedged between the bar and a dark alleyway.

He'd talk to Brody tomorrow morning. Holt had no idea what he'd say yet. Maybe just relay the exchange between himself and Edward Thompson.

He pulled out his phone and called his dad. Neal Dalton answered on the third ring, his trademark.

"Thanks for the warning about the hothead, Dad." Seriously. Neal Dalton couldn't have given him a heads-up that some loose cannon was on his way?

"I'm sure you handled it fine, Holt."

"How, exactly, am I supposed to handle it? Brody's eighteen and so is Thompson's daughter. Oh and by the way—if I don't break up the relationship, he threatened to pull his big donation to the ranchers' association and make sure the powers that be know it's our fault."

"Classic," Neal said with almost respect in his voice. Whose side was his dad on?

"I'll talk to Brody in the morning when he turns up. Though I don't know why you sent Thompson to me when he was already at your house and you could have dealt with him."

"Because I figured you could talk him down, use your own experience but with hindsight, you know? I don't always have the answers even if I think I know everything."

Maybe his dad was coming around some. There didn't even seem to be a back-handed compliment in that. And good thing because Holt hated clapping back at his dad, hating being at odds with the man. Getting along meant the world to his mother, and Holt knew it.

"I'll see what I can do, Dad."

Which would clearly not include trying to explain to Edward Thompson that Holt couldn't stop his daughter from dating who she wanted. He'd tried that, and it was beside the point for Thompson. The *point* was separating the couple. Keeping Piper Thompson "uncorrupted." Making sure she left for college in three weeks, the Bronco Valley "punk" history.

Well, he couldn't blame his dad for thinking Holt knew something about that very topic.

"Kiss Robby good-night for me," his dad said and hung up.

Holt shook his head. His father made him want to throw something. He walked down the porch steps into the front yard and threw a stick as hard as he could. Bentley went flying after it, returning it and dropping it at his feet.

"Good dog," Holt said, giving Bentley's side a pat. Yup, that was what happened when you tried to avoid something, throw it away. It came right back, demanding to be dealt with.

Like Amanda maybe. She'd come back into his life for a reason. Now. Just when he was ready for her. That had to mean something.

He went back to the porch swing, Bentley trailing after him. Thompson had gotten under his skin and Holt knew why. Because in a parallel universe, the man could have easily been Amanda's father, furious about Holt and Amanda, and deep down Holt still felt like that twenty-two-year-old guy.

He'd changed his ways because of Robby, and seven years later, he led the most law-abiding, kid-focused life possible. His world was work and Robby and his family whereas ten years ago, before Amanda and in the few years after, his life had been about chasing a good time, pretty women and cold beer. His group of friends at the time were just like him. One had ended up in prison for a string of burglaries. Another had joined the army and had probably been straightened out. And another had tried to turn his life around when his older brother died of a drug overdose and had had to leave Whitehorn because no one would let him change, be a new person.

Sometimes Holt thought his dad didn't accept that he'd changed. Neal Dalton acted like Holt could revert at any time.

I coulda sworn you married that hard-edged gal because you knocked her up, his father had said at his and Sally Anne's wedding. *But she says she's not expecting.*

I married her because I love her, Holt had said.

He had loved Sally Anne. Yeah, she was rough around the edges—just like he was. They came from the same place, so to speak. They spoke the same language, understood each other. But Sally Anne had been even wilder than Holt, and she lived for attention.

What killed Holt now, and during the past four years since he'd been raising his son on his own, was that Holt's choices had put Robby in this position. To have a mother who'd walked out on him. To need his reading tutor to stand in at a mother-son fun run. To wonder why he wasn't special enough for his own mother to want to be in his life. Sometimes Holt thought about what his dad had said at the wedding and regretted not knowing better, not making sure that a woman who'd said she wasn't maternal, wasn't cut out for motherhood didn't get pregnant by accident. They'd been young and in love and tipsy most of the time—and careless.

Anyway, if Holt hadn't married Sally Anne, Robby wouldn't exist. And Holt wouldn't trade his life with his son for anything.

He got up and headed back inside with Bentley, giving Oliver his dinner reserve, which had the cat rushing over, then he shut the lights on the first floor. He, Bentley and Oliver went upstairs, Bentley going back into Robby's room and Oliver following Holt into his own bedroom. Usually the cat stuck with Bentley, but Holt was glad for the company tonight.

He sat down on the edge of his bed and opened the bottom drawer of his end table as Oliver jumped up on his bed and scratched at a spot and then curled up. Under a bunch of old keepsakes was one of the most precious of all: a photo of him and Amanda from ten years ago. They were sitting on the dock of the lake at Camp KidPower, Amanda's back against his chest, her legs straight out in front of him, his arms wrapped around her. They were both beaming. And so damned young.

He wondered what the story was with Brody and Piper, if they were in love like he and Amanda had been. Maybe Brody already planned to walk away from Piper, to let her head off to school and start her new life, which had no place for him. Or maybe the two had other ideas. In any case, they were adults, new ones but legally able to make their own decisions whether Thompson approved or not.

Holt would talk to Brody in the morning but he had to wonder: how could he advise Brody to walk away from Piper for her own good when doing exactly that with Amanda was the biggest mistake Holt had ever made?

Chapter Ten

The next morning, Amanda was happy to see her next-door neighbor Melanie Driscoll come out of her apartment as Amanda was leaving and locking up. Mel spent a lot of time at her fiancé's ranch, so Amanda didn't get to see her dear friend as often as she used to. As usual lately, Amanda's gaze went right to Mel's gorgeous diamond engagement ring.

What did *that* mean? Amanda used to be drawn to the ring kind of wistfully, as in, *That'll never happen for me because I've taken myself out of the game.* Now, the ring seemed to say something else to her. *I symbolize love and commitment and those things really do exist.*

Maybe Amanda *was* changing? Just a little? She hoped so. Being closed and guarded didn't feel great.

Amanda smiled at her friend, who looked beautiful as always. Mel's long blond hair was loose past her shoulders, and she wore the cutest outfit. Amanda glanced at her own outfit, which was professional meets superdull. She loved the way Mel and Brittany dressed with style and flair, but Amanda had always been a more fade-into-the-woodwork type. Maybe she'd ask Mel and Brittany to go shopping with her and let them suggest some upgrades to her ho-hum look.

The funny thing—and funny strange, not funny ha-ha—was that Holt seemed to find her sexy just as she was. He had ten years ago, too, which had shocked not only her but all the girls at camp. Amanda of the ponytail, no makeup, baggy T-shirts, and nose in a book had somehow stolen the attention of the cutest guy in camp. Once, when a girl asked Holt what he saw in her—Amanda had happened to be in eavesdropping distance but not visible—she'd heard Holt respond, *I see everything in Amanda—everything beautiful and everything that matters.* The girl had swooned. Amanda had burst into tears, unable to believe that someone, someone she'd fallen so hard for, had said something like that about her. She'd wanted to call her mom and tell her, but her mother wasn't the kind you shared stuff like that with. Amanda had held it close to her heart until he'd dumped her, when she'd stopped believing in anything Holt had said to her.

A few weeks into camp, Amanda had made a close girlfriend, another counselor who also had a boyfriend she was nuts about, and the two girls had told each everything. Daniella had been always been there for her over the years, and though she now lived in Alaska, Amanda would always feel close to her faraway friend. In fact, Daniella had paved the way for Amanda to open up to new girlfriends, and she'd easily become close to Brittany in college and then Mel when she moved next door. She trusted in girlfriends. Not so much boyfriends.

"Hi, Mel. I've been meaning to update you on my online search for Beatrix. So far, no leads on the one site I posted to—adoptees looking for information—but last night I posted on two other sites. I'm so hopeful."

"Me too," Mel said. "I want to find Beatrix so badly."

"You'll find her. I truly believe that."

Her own words shocked her. Maybe instead of

being so cynical, she was becoming more open to possibilities. She hoped so. She certainly wasn't looking to get hurt again, but her wise room-mate's words kept coming back to her. *Keep an open mind—even just a smidge open.*

Did she dare do that when she was entering a race called the Mother-Son Fun Run with Holt's child? She already felt close to Robby Dalton. Being involved in something like this, given Robby's par-ticular situation, pulled her in even more. She'd love to have a little boy just like Robby. But the thought of giving Holt another chance felt…scary. Truly scary. To allow herself to be that vulnerable, and then to be left heartbroken and alone… She couldn't do it. She wouldn't do it. She had a plan for a Robby of her own. She was researching, in-vestigating, figuring out.

Amanda and Mel headed out into the perfect August Montana morning together, chatting about the search for Beatrix, then went their separate ways. Amanda couldn't stop thinking about Jo-siah Abernathy and Winona Cobbs during the short walk to the coffee shop, where she picked up an iced mocha latte to fortify herself for her presentation to a potential new client. Somewhere out there, a seventy-five-year-old woman may have been wondering about her birth parents all these years. That was if Beatrix even knew she'd been adopted at birth.

Amanda had so many questions. Had Josiah kept tabs on his baby girl from afar? He'd known where she was. Now, with Josiah suffering from Alzheimer's, he was unable to provide any answers about the past. It was up to Mel and the great search.

An hour later, after Amanda's meeting with the school district's superintendent about potentially taking on their social media needs, she stopped back in the coffee shop with her laptop to type up her notes and to work on a few other current campaigns. One thing she loved about her job was that she could do it anywhere. Such as while drinking a sweet iced tea and nibbling on a white chocolate and raspberry scone.

"CJ Donville is supercute," a voice whispered from the table beside her. "And omigosh, did you see that blond guy with the serious muscles at the health club last night? Hot!"

Amanda smiled to herself. She loved girl talk—even just listening. She'd noticed the two women, neither of whom she'd recognized, when she'd sat down. Both were in their midtwenties, one blond with great bangs, the other auburn-haired with killer eyebrows.

"I have my eye on a few Dalton brothers," the redhead said.

Amanda almost spit out her iced tea. Suddenly, she wasn't so sure she wanted to be hearing this.

The blonde nodded. "Five gorgeous brothers! Holt is so hot, but forget him. And Morgan—ooh la la. Ridiculously sexy. You should go for him."

Forget Holt? Why? Because he was involved with someone, namely Amanda? No one would know that, though. But they *had* been spending time together around town—Bronco's Brick Oven Pizza just last night. Maybe people thought they were a couple.

No, other women didn't look at Amanda and think the hottest guy in town would go for *her*.

The redhead shook her head and bit into her bagel. "Do you know Cheyenne, the junior Realtor at Bronco Properties? Tall, thin, huge chest, gorgeous? She has guys chasing her left and right. She asked Morgan out after running into him in the grocery store and he turned her down, made some excuse. So trust me, Morgan's no better."

No better? What did *that* mean?

"Yeah, neither of them seems to be interested in anyone right now," the blonde said, then sipped her drink. "I thought Holt stopped dating because no one could deal with his hyper kid."

Amanda narrowed her eyes. Hyper? How dare

she refer to Robby in an unkind manner! Kids were off-limits—worldwide rule.

"No, I heard he's seeing someone," the friend said.

Amanda had no doubt that someone *was* her. Might not be true, but she did like the idea of Holt being off the market. And clearly there was quite a market.

The blonde smirked. "Like that'll last. My cousin Lulu dated Holt last year when he first moved to town. He's gorgeous and a total gentleman, but he's a package deal and his kid's a nightmare. Never stops talking and has to be the center of attention. Holt told Lulu his son has to be his priority, not dating."

Amanda wanted to take her iced tea and dump it over the woman's head, then crumble the scone on top. What gossips! How dare they!

"Well, shouldn't his child have priority over his love life?" the redhead asked. "I think that's a good thing."

"I guess. He told Lulu he's looking for a mother for his son. She heard that and ran for the hills. Holt is seriously hot, but she knew she'd turn into the babysitter real quick and have the life sucked out of her. No thanks. No one needs a brat aging them ten years in a month! Who could afford that kind of Botox upkeep?"

The women laughed and clinked to that with a double amen.

Steam coming out of her ears, despite the air-conditioning in the coffee shop, Amanda packed up her laptop, stuffed her half-eaten scone into its little bag and into her tote and grabbed her tea. She stood up and turned to the women. "You're talking about a seven-year-old boy. And before you tell me to mind my own business, maybe consider that when you gossip about people in a coffee shop, you never know who's sitting next to you."

Both women's mouths dropped open. Amanda stalked out, fury climbing up her spine.

She was halfway down the block before it occurred to her that the old Amanda—Amanda of even a week ago—would never have spoken up like that. She would have been too shy and instead would have spent all night tossing and turning and thinking of comebacks she wished she could have been confident enough to hurl back at those hyenas in lip gloss.

You are *changing*, she realized, a smile forming on her lips.

Her phone pinged with a text. It was from Holt, and the way her heart leaped made her doubly sure she was changing, that she was letting him in. If just a smidge.

Robby woke up asking if it was all a dream, that he would get to be in the Mother-Son Fun Run with you. I assured him it was real. Thank you, thank you, thank you.

He'd added the emoji of a smiley face wearing a cowboy hat.

Amanda brought her hand to her heart, so touched she almost cried.

She was in deep trouble.

Holt had checked Brody Colter's schedule for the morning. The cowboy was on herding duty till eleven, then would be meeting the shipment of feed at eleven thirty. Holt planned to catch him right after the truck left. The two could stack the heavy bags—and talk.

Right on time, Holt saw the young hand loping his way to the barn, a metal water bottle in his hand. Neal Dalton had commented on Brody's good posture when he'd signed off on hiring him; his dad took that as a sign of something good. Holt watched the tall, lanky blonde swish his mop of bangs out of the way, then take a long drink and stuff the bottle in his backpack and grab a cereal bar, which he'd finished by the time the truck pulled in. Holt nodded at Brody and helped unload the truck, which seemed to surprise the cowboy. The Dalton guys didn't usually do the gruntiest of grunt labor.

"Brody, I'm gonna just come out with this," Holt said, grabbing a huge feed sack from the stack.

The guy whirled to him, alarm on his face. "I do something wrong?"

"I had a visit last night from Edward Thompson."

Brody's face fell and he let out a breath.

"He wants me to convince you to break up with his daughter for her own good," Holt said. "If not, he won't make his usual big donation to the ranchers' association and he'll blame Dalton's Grange for that."

Brody lifted his chin, squinting under the brim of his cowboy hat. "I'm not breaking up with Piper. She's stood up to her father ever since he found out about us. She was strong enough to do that, there's no way I'll let her down by walking away."

Good for you, kid, Holt thought. "You'd lose your job over Piper?" He headed into the barn and laid the bag of feed on the big pallet.

"You'd fire me?" Brody shot back, following him with another bag of feed.

The kid had conviction and Holt liked him. He also had a feeling Brody knew Holt wouldn't fire him. Dalton's Grange had a good reputation in town, despite the family only being in Bronco a year. The Daltons were known for being honest, even if some of the snobbier types in Bronco Heights referred to them as "new money." Holt had never understood why that was an insult; it meant someone came from nothing and made something of themselves. Granted, Neal Dalton had done that at the casino, but he was putting his blood, sweat and tears, and everything he was, into the ranch. Holt had learned long ago that it was what you did with your opportunities that counted.

Holt had thrown an opportunity named Amanda right out the window, hadn't he? He hadn't seen the situation with the same eyes he did now. If he had, he might have viewed his relationship with Amanda as a partnership, been honest with her, gotten her take on things. Instead, he'd basically lied about who he was and then made decisions for them. At least he could say he was young then. Now, he wouldn't squander an opportunity he knew was a good thing.

"Touché, Brody," he said as they headed back to the stack outside. "And no, I won't fire you. I don't like threats or ultimatums. You work for Dalton's Grange and that makes us Team Brody. We've got your back."

The cowboy's face broke into relief. "Really?"

Holt hefted another bag. "Yeah, really. Sounds like you really care about this young woman."

Brody nodded and grabbed a bag, balancing it over his shoulder. "I love her more than anything. She's the best thing that's ever happened to me. Piper makes me want to be better in every aspect of my life, you know?"

He did know. That was how he'd felt about Amanda ten years ago.

Brody was quiet for a minute as they finished getting the bags of feed into the barn.

"But her father thinks I'm a loser from the wrong side of the tracks," Brody continued, taking off his hat and using a bandanna from his pocket to wipe his forehead. "And I know that for a fact because I overheard him say so after I dropped her off at home one night. He kept asking Piper what she could possibly see in a ranch hand who smelled like cattle and was going nowhere in life."

Holt shook his head. "He's got you figured out at eighteen? Please."

Brody brightened some, clearly appreciating that Holt was on his side.

"A long time ago I once dated a girl from another world," Holt said. "I never felt like I had anything to offer her and that was wrong. I broke up with her because I thought she deserved better. I had no faith in myself at all. I'm glad you do, Brody."

"I don't know where it comes from. My mom died two years ago, and the day before my eighteenth birthday almost a year ago now, my father told me he was taking off with his girlfriend in her RV and they had no idea where they'd end up. It's why I live in that tiny one-room hovel above Wild Wesley's. I work there part-time, sweeping and mopping and loading the dishwashers."

So he didn't hang out in dive bars, like Edward Thompson had said. He worked there when he already had a full-time job on the ranch.

"That fight you got in—the one I bailed you out of jail for," Holt said. "You got caught in the middle of something?"

"I was bussing a table and some jerk said something really sexist to a waitress, so I told him that he was rude and he slugged me but missed, but then came after me. He was so drunk he kept missing, but I hit him once to get him off me and he called the cops."

Holt doubted Thompson would care about the details. "If you need more hours, Brody, I can take care of that. You can stay an extra hour every day or work a few on the weekends—whatever you want."

"Really?" Brody asked, brightening again.

"That'd be great. It would probably help with Piper's dad if I didn't work there anymore. She told him I had two jobs because I'm hardworking and want to build a nest egg to buy my own small ranch, and I heard him laugh and say a guy like me will never get past minimum wage and we were both kidding ourselves."

Edward Thompson was a real jerk.

Holt shook his head. "I have no doubt you'll achieve your dreams, Brody. That's what goals and hard work are about."

"Hope so," Brody said.

"Thompson said Piper's been saying she might not go to college after all. That seems to be what has him all riled up."

Brody looked off at the mountains for a second, then turned back to Holt. "She's afraid the distance will come between us, but I keep telling her we're too solid for anything to get in our way. I think she should go to college and that I should join the army—like my dad and uncle did after high school. My goal has always been to have my own ranch one day, but I like the idea of serving my country too. Piper can go to school for four years like she planned and I'll serve. Then we'll get married and start our lives together."

That also sounded solid to Holt. But Brody was biting his lip and looking away.

"Except?" Holt prompted.

"Except Piper doesn't want me going away for four years. She suggested I follow her to college and get a live-in job on a ranch nearby, but there aren't many ranches out there. She thinks we should buy a piece of land and start our own small homestead with like ten head of cattle and some sheep and chickens. She wants to make her own cheese and yogurt."

Holt smiled. "And what do you think of that idea?"

"I think it sounds like a fairy tale. Piper's the best, but she grew up in a fancy house in Bronco Heights and hasn't had to make milk or cheese to sell in order to have money for the power bill or groceries." His shoulders sagged. "Before I started working at the bar, I didn't have much left after paying my bills and ate those foam cups of noodle soup for a few days. Piper doesn't know what that's like and I don't want her to."

Holt nodded. "I think your idea of Piper going to school and you into the service is a great one, Brody. That'll let you both grow up some. You can remain committed as a couple. That's up to you two."

"That's what I think too. I just have to make her see it's the best plan for both of us. She seems to think I'm trying to end things. I just want her to have everything. And throwing away college and pissing off her dad isn't having everything."

"You're smart and focused, Brody. And it's admirable that you want her to stay on good terms with her dad. You two just need to get on the same page about where to go from here."

"What if we can't agree?"

Holt thought about that for a second. "Well, you know one thing for sure—you want to be together. Just keep that as the baseline. Whatever you do, make sure all roads lead to that."

"Mr. Thompson wants me out of Piper's life altogether. I hate coming between her and her father."

Holt really felt for Brody. He was in a tough situation and basically alone.

"Brody, help me for a sec," another ranch hand called.

"Coming," Brody said to him.

"Sorry to get mixed up in your business," Holt said. "Just know if you need to talk to someone, I'm here for you. And I mean it about the extra hours."

Brody smiled. "Thanks," he said, and walked toward the other cowboy, shoulders down, pressed by a weight that shouldn't be there.

Holt knew Edward Thompson was going to try to get his way here, and that things were going to get ugly. For *who*, exactly, in the end, Holt wasn't sure.

What was certain was that Brody was going to put Piper first. Holt had always thought that was what he was doing when he left Amanda a decade ago, but now he realized the opposite was true.

He hadn't been one-tenth the man Brody was now. Holt hadn't been putting Amanda first at all; he'd been afraid she'd discover who he really was out of that magical camp setting and everything would come falling down on his head. He'd believed who he really was wouldn't measure up and so he'd walked away. To save himself—not her.

He understood that now. And these few past days he thought he just needed to prove to Amanda that he'd changed. But *had* he changed?

The past ten years he hadn't been successful at anything. Yeah, he had a kid he loved. But Holt was a father who'd been told his son wasn't welcome back at camp because of his behavior. And Holt was a son who'd never figured out how to have a relationship with his father—and that relationship was now at an all-time low. And workwise? Here he was, working for someone else. His family, though, and he did like that more than he'd ever realized. Still, he'd never started his own ranch, which had once been his dream.

He hadn't made anything of himself in all these years. Not at home or at work or in love.

He was trying for a second chance with Amanda? Damn, maybe he should back the hell off. In fact, he'd do just that.

This time around he *was* going to put Amanda Jenkins first.

Chapter Eleven

The Mother-Son Fun Run started at eight o'clock and was located in a park close to Amanda's apartment building, so she let Holt know she'd meet him and Robby there. She could barely wait. She hadn't seen either Dalton yesterday. She'd planned on going over to tutor Robby as usual but Holt had canceled, saying "something came up." Amanda had always thought that was code for "making something up to get out of plans." If Holt had said Robby had a dentist appointment or he had a buddy coming over or a terribly tummy ache, she would have believed it.

Something came up. Humph. Something *was* up was more like it. But why would he want to stop her from coming over? She spent her time with Robby—not Holt. Maybe he'd explain this morning.

When she arrived at the park, the sight of all those mothers and boys in their matching race T-shirts almost took her breath. If Amanda was lucky, one day, she'd have two boys and two girls. But right now, she got to stand in as mom, and the idea gave her a little jolt of joy.

"Amanda!"

She turned to find Robby racing full speed ahead toward her. He slowed down a bit, thank heavens, before wrapping his arms around her. "Morning, partner!" she said, giving him a hug back.

He beamed up at her.

Holt was making his way over, weaving through the crowds, his expression neutral. What was going on with him?

"I'm so excited!" Robby said, taking her attention, for which she was glad. She'd spent way too many hard nights analyzing Holt Dalton, and she had to put a stop to it.

"Me too!" she said, giving Robby a high five. They'd both already picked up their registration packets from the town hall the other day and had their race shirts and bib numbers pinned on. The last three numbers were the same to show they were a pair.

As Holt joined them, Amanda could see he was definitely subdued. Maybe he'd had a run-in with his dad yesterday and that was why he'd canceled. Or a tough afternoon with Robby? Single parenting couldn't be easy; Amanda had no experience in that, but she wasn't kidding herself that it would be good times 24/7. In any case, she should stop speculating. Ten years ago, when he'd left her and hadn't looked back, she'd had no choice but to wonder about what had been going on in his head. Now, he was right here. All she had to do was ask if she wanted honesty about why he'd canceled. And why he seemed so...distant now. Subtle, but she could see it in his face and feel it in the air around them.

"That's the start line," Robby said, pointing at the huge banner across the grass. "And on the way back it becomes the finish line."

Amanda eyed the mile-long loop and hoped she didn't conk out halfway. She wasn't a runner and didn't belong to a gym. Her exercise came from walking around town—which, come to think of it, probably didn't count as exercise. Hey, at least it was something physical.

As Robby was talking about their matching

T-shirts and race bibs, a boy standing nearby turned and stared at him. He looked to be around Robby's age.

"Why are you here, Robby?" the boy asked, freckles dotting his cheeks.

"Same as you, Ethan!" Robby said, pointing to his blue sneakers. "I'm running."

Ethan tilted his head. "Yeah, but you don't have a mom. How can you run in the mother-son race if you don't have a mom?"

Amanda's stomach flip-flopped. Kids came out with whatever was on their minds. She glanced at Holt, who stood ramrod straight, his gaze on his son, whose expression had gone from happy and excited to sad and defeated.

"I have a mom," Robby said, frowning.

"No," Ethan insisted.

"Yes. She just lives far away."

The boy scrunched up his face. "That's weird."

"*You're* weird!" Robby said, and went to push the boy, but Holt clearly knew his son and scooped him up and away before he could.

"What is going on here?" asked a woman who looked a lot like Ethan.

"Robby said I was weird," the boy said, and stuck out his tongue.

"Mrs. Anderson said kids should mind their own business!" Robby shouted, tears in his eyes.

"Mrs. Anderson isn't our teacher anymore," Ethan said, his mother pulling him away.

Amanda shook her head. "Why don't we wait on the other side of the lineup?"

"Good idea," Holt said, and they moved a few feet away. Holt looked angry, Robby was about to cry, and Amanda's heart was breaking for the little guy.

"Is Ethan right?" Robby asked his father, tears falling down his face. "I can't run the race cuz I don't really have a mom?"

"Hey," Holt said, kneeling in front of him. "You saw the race rules—'mom' means anyone who feels like a mom. Someone special in your life who's kind and helps. Do you know some-one like that?"

"Amanda's like that," Robby said, swiping under his eyes with his forearm.

Holt gently pushed Robby's bangs out of his eyes. "Right. So there's no problem with you run-ning the race."

"There kind of is, Daddy," Robby said. The tears fell harder and Amanda bit her lip. "Why doesn't my mom want to live where I live?"

Holt glanced at Amanda, and she could plainly see the pain in his eyes. He looked at his son and put his hands on Robby's little shoulders. "I wish

I understood that myself, Robby. Because you're the best kid in the world."

That seemed to make Robby feel better. "But I always get in trouble. Is that why my mom doesn't come to see me?"

Oh Robby, Amanda thought.

"Robby Dalton, I promise you that you're a great kid, the very best I know. The reasons your mom lives far away don't have anything to do with you. That is the truest thing I know."

Amanda stared at Holt in wonder. She was so moved by his honesty and how he didn't try to change the subject. He was answering his son's questions the best way he knew how—questions that didn't have answers.

Robby was staring at the ground.

"I agree with your dad, Robby. You're a great kid."

Robby glanced up at Amanda and a smile broke out on his face.

"The race is gonna start soon," Holt said. "But if you don't feel like participating, that's okay."

"Do you still want to run with me, Amanda?" Robby asked.

She reached out her hand and he put his little one in hers. "You bet I do. I can't wait. This will be my very first race. Let's get to the start line!"

"I hope I'm faster than Ethan."

Amanda smiled and tapped his nose. "Ooh, I just thought of something. How about after this we go out for a special brunch? My treat."

Holt was staring at her. Uh-oh. She'd gotten so caught up with Robby that she wasn't thinking about the fact that Holt didn't want her in his orbit for some reason. But then his expression softened. "French toast sound good to me."

"Pancakes," Robby said. "Chocolate chip ones. And bacon."

"That's what I'm having too," Amanda said.

Robby was smiling and excited again.

"You know, Robby," Holt said, kneeling down in front of his son again, "I like the way you handled that conversation with Ethan. Except I got the feeling you were about to push him. You might have thought he deserved it because he wasn't being kind, but pushing someone is wrong. Same with hitting. Right?"

"Yeah. But I did want to push him *and* hit him. Teachers always say 'use your words,' but sometimes I don't know what to say."

"I completely understand," Holt said. "When you feel that way, just walk away. You can find me and we can talk it over, or if you're at school, you can tell your teacher."

"'Kay, Daddy."

"Family hug?" Holt said, holding out his arms.

Robby flung himself at his father, and Amanda realized just how much she wished she could be part of that family hug—and how attached she was to both Daltons.

A whistle blew and then a man's voice could be heard over a megaphone. "Time to line up, moms and sons!"

"That's us!" Amanda said, taking Robby's hand. "Ready?"

The smile on Robby's face almost made Amanda cry. "Ready!"

Amanda glanced at Holt, but again, he seemed…distant. Something was bothering him. Something that might have been exacerbated by what had just happened.

"See you two at the finish line," Holt said. "I'll be cheering you on."

The whistle blew again and the runners were off. Amanda felt like part of her heart was right beside her and the other part waiting at the finish line.

Holt had been prepared for his son to want to talk about his mother during brunch, but Robby hadn't brought up Sally Anne once, and now the three of them—Holt, Robby and Amanda—were just about finished with brunch. On one hand, Holt was relieved the subject hadn't come up; on the other, maybe he himself should have asked Robby outright if he had questions or wanted to talk about his mother. Waiting for cues from Robby had always been the way Holt had handled the topic, but maybe that was wrong. Maybe Holt should ask. He wished he had all the answers, all the right answers—to his own questions and to Robby's—but he didn't.

And maybe talking in front of Amanda wouldn't have been a good idea, anyway, though she seemed comfortable with the conversation in the park. She'd let him handle it, which he appreciated, and when she had joined in, it had been to back him up that Robby was a great kid, which he'd also appreciated.

During brunch, his son had been focused on talking about the run—that he'd finished without stopping, that he passed by that "mean Ethan Snowling" and that it was one of his favorite days of his entire life, maybe only after adopting Bentley and Oliver.

Because he'd had a "mom" for the morning? Because he'd simply had a fun time with his tutor, who he liked very much, his dad cheering them on?

Holt had thought he should distance himself from Amanda, that he should put any notion of a second chance out of his head, but maybe he had it wrong again. As he'd watched the mile-long race, Amanda and Robby running their hearts out, Robby smiling, focused, happy, Amanda so damned beautiful without a shred of makeup, her hair in a ponytail, wearing the bright blue race T-shirt, a thought had hit him. Hard. Their wants and needs were in perfect alignment.

Amanda wanted a child. He wanted a mother for Robby. Maybe the two of them finding what they needed in each other was the answer. Amanda had said she was done with love. And hell, maybe he was too. He didn't want to be, but after his marriage fiasco and trying to date to find Robby a good mom, he'd backed way off from trying to find a life partner.

They could both get they wanted. What they needed.

He'd just have to show her that she could trust him, that he was the guy she'd always thought he was.

The race had ended in a snap, so he'd had to put his thoughts out of his head so he could drive them all to the café without crashing into a pole. He'd done a good job of focusing on his breakfast companions, but now he was back to wondering. Was it possible—

"Earth to Holt, earth to Holt."

He started, realizing Amanda was talking to him.

Robby giggled and put down his little glass of orange juice. "Daddy, Amanda was saying your name but you were in another world like people say about me when I'm not paying attention to them. You were probably thinking of something really good, right?"

He smiled—and wanted to reach over and hug his son hard. "Yeah, I was thinking of something good." He turned to Amanda. "Sorry. What were you saying?"

"Hey, aren't those your brothers? See—by the painting of the dog with the cowboy hat on?"

Holt looked over and squinted. Huh. Dale and Shep were just getting up from their table. "Yup, you're right. Hey, Robby. I see your uncles over there. Wanna go say hi?"

Robby leaped up and raced over before Holt could remind him to walk. Luckily, a waitress with a tray of full plates wasn't anywhere in his path.

Holt tried to put cash on the table but Amanda reminded him this was her idea and her treat, and he relented. When the group met up at the door, Shep and Dale said they were headed to watch a rodeo competition a few towns over and invited Robby, who practically catapulted onto the ceiling in excitement—an opportunity to see Daring Drake. Holt took off Robby's race bib, and off the boy went with his uncles. Again, Holt was grateful that he'd moved to Bronco so that his son would have a big family who loved spending time with him.

Now he was also grateful he'd moved here because of Amanda.

"Take a walk?" he asked her. He bit his lip, wondering if he should come right out with his idea about them. It was a big deal, though, and something he should think over. He held open the door and out they went into the warm, bright sunshine.

"You're cutting me out, aren't you," she said, a statement, not a question. She stood stock-still, staring at him. "You canceled yesterday and you seemed conflicted this morning—before the conversation with Robby, I mean."

Since they were smack in the middle of town, he kept seeing people he knew and so did Amanda, so they decided to talk in his truck. Once they were both settled, he said, "I'm going to be honest with what's on my mind."

"Good," she said.

"You said you were done with love and romance, but I kept thinking maybe I could have a second chance here. But then I realized that I don't deserve it. I was selfish ten years ago— walking away from our relationship to protect myself. Not you, myself. I didn't want to get found out for the imposter I was."

She seemed to be taking that in. "Okay, I get that. But that was a decade ago. Now is another story. You're distancing yourself because…?"

He stared out the windshield, then turned to her. "I was thinking I should because nothing in my life is working out right now, Amanda. Relationships haven't worked out—from my marriage to the women I've dated the past year. I need to focus on Robby—get him more settled before school starts. I need to be more present for him, too, as evidenced by this morning and the conversation before the race about his mother. I need to focus on him. And I need to fix my problems with my dad—somehow."

"So, canceling a tutoring and babysitting session with me is helping Robby? I'm part of that 'get him settled' before school starts."

"Well, thinking I should back off from you was before I realized the opposite is true."

She narrowed her eyes. "What are you talking about exactly?"

Just come out with it, he told himself. *You don't risk, you don't get*. That was the damned truth. He looked at her, bracing himself. "I'm just saying let's give this a real shot, Amanda."

"Give what a shot—a relationship?"

He nodded. "You want a child. And you adore Robby. I need a wonderful, loving mother for him. Someone I trust. Neither of us is looking for…someone else to give us what we need. So… why not give us a chance?"

She was staring at him as though he'd grown an extra head. "You're serious, aren't you?"

"Very. I want to do what's right and best for Robby. That seems to perfectly align with what you want, Amanda."

Tears shimmered in her eyes. Oh hell. Did he mess this up?

"What are you thinking?" he asked gently.

"I'm thinking I don't know. That I just need to go think—alone."

"I understand." He didn't want her to get out of the truck. He just wanted her close.

"So, basically, Holt, you're asking me out. On a date. I mean, if we're gonna start something, it's gotta start with that first date."

A date. Yes. "We can see how it feels to be together on a date. And that date can be anything you want it to be, Amanda. We can take Bentley for a long walk and just talk and hang out. We can go out to dinner and share a bottle of wine. We can sit on the sofa and watch Marvel movies."

"You mean rom-coms," she said, sending him a half smile.

There was hope here. He could tell. "I'll watch any lovey-dovey movie you want."

She glanced out the window, then turned to him. "I'm not saying no. Or yes. I need to think about this, Holt." She took a deep breath. "I'll take the weekend to think about it. I'll be over Monday to tutor Robby and babysit. We can talk afterward, okay?"

How would he get through the weekend not knowing if she'd say yes?

"I'm just asking for a chance, Amanda. To show you who I am now."

She looked at him and he knew by her expression, by her eyes that she was halfway to yes already. She wanted a second chance just like he did, but after how he'd treated her, after getting left at the altar in her wedding dress, she was afraid to try again, afraid to even believe in love. She might say no, that dating—even one date—was out of the question.

"See you Monday," she said, getting out of the truck.

He wished she was still beside him.

Chapter Twelve

"Of course you're going on a date!" Brittany said. "And please, I'm not talking a dog walk in the woods in your unsexy hiking sandals. I'm talking Dinner. Candles. Wine. A good-night kiss…"

Amanda and her roommate were sitting on the balcony of their building, Amanda staring off at the mountains in the distance. She'd told Brittany every detail of the morning and conversation with Holt after brunch. When Amanda had gotten home, she'd tried to do some work but couldn't concentrate, and was grateful when her wise and insightful roommate had come in.

Amanda took a sip of her iced tea and stared out at the view, hoping the beautiful vistas would provide all the answers. No such luck. "I don't know how to just let go of everything I've been through, though. I don't trust anymore, Brittany. And I don't believe love even exists."

"I know it's not easy to put yourself out there. Especially with a guy who broke your heart. But love *definitely* exists. Case in point, our neighbor Mel, who's rarely home these days because she's with Gabe—and those two are big time in love. Ferociously so."

That was true. The early days of Mel's relationship with Gabriel Abernathy had been anything but "love at first sight" and happy-ever-after. They'd fought hard for how strongly they felt for each other, despite their issues. And love won.

Her roommate sipped her own drink, then pushed her long curls behind her shoulders. "Holt Dalton is asking you for a chance. And *one* date to see. A baby step. If you're at the restaurant and looking at him across the candlelit table with some soft music playing and you feel like throwing up, fine—then you're not meant to be dating him or anyone. But at least *see*."

Amanda knew she wouldn't feel remotely nauseated or the slightest bit of dread if she were sitting across from Holt, both of them dressed up for a date. Butterflies, sure. But in a good way. Because Holt was so good-looking, so sexy, and he was part of her past and a big part of her present; she was already wrapped up in his life. So much so that she'd run a mother-son race with his son.

That was the problem, though. Being so invested in his life. The good butterflies. The real date. Everything that would be between them in that restaurant and hovering in the air. She'd have a taste of romance with Holt and be drawn right back in. Then down the line, whether two dates later or a few months, she'd be dumped again. *It's not you, it's me. This just isn't working out. I thought we could be what we each needed, but I was wrong...*

That was what she was afraid of. So why try at all? Why go on that one date when she'd end up with a broken heart, ugly-crying for days and eating Ben & Jerry's out of the container in bed with Poindexter?

She said exactly that to Brittany.

"And here I thought I was stubborn," her roommate said. "Honey, I don't get serious about the men I date because I'm not looking to be a wife and mama. You *are*. Everything you want, deep in your heart—which includes love and romance and happily-ever-after and a child—is possible with Holt Dalton. And I'll just come right out with this—the man you never stopped loving."

That was definitely true. "And if he hurts me again?" Amanda asked, biting her lip. She pictured herself waiting in a hotel room in Las Vegas, the veil she'd splurged on with the delicate beading that had reminded her of something Audrey Hepburn would have worn, her groom never appearing. *Holt*—never appearing.

She'd be knocked to her knees.

"Then, Amanda Jenkins," Brittany said, sitting up very straight and looking at her pointedly, "I'll be there to see you through the heartache, and in time, you'll open yourself up to going through it all over again because that's life. Love is everything."

"But not for you?" Amanda asked.

"Hey, I've got nothing against love. I just don't want marriage and kids. Right now. Maybe not ever. I don't know."

"Why is the subject of love so damned complicated?" Amanda asked with a sigh.

"Right?" Brittany said.

They clinked their iced tea glasses and sat in silence, looking out at the breathtaking view.

Amanda heard a sexy giggle, then a male voice say, "C'mere you." She turned to see that her next-door neighbor, Mel, and her fiancé had come out onto the adjacent balcony, locked in a very passionate kiss, eyes closed, arms wrapped around each other as they edged toward the railing.

"Um, don't fall over," Brittany called over, shooting Amanda a grin.

Mel opened an eye, her mouth forming an O at being caught in a hot PDA, before Gabe reclaimed her lips, taking off his cowboy hat and holding it to the side to shield the lovebirds from view.

Amanda and Brittany both laughed, but inside, Amanda was deep-sighing wistfully. That sure did bring back memories—of her two big romances and some littler ones. Love, desire, romance.

Dammit, she wanted in.

"I know what you need, Holt."

He glanced toward the voice—his dad's. Why did he doubt that Neal Dalton thought he knew what he needed?

Holt looked back down at the new-hire checklist on his iPad and clicked the first two boxes as the cowboy-trainee they'd hired mucked out the big pen at the far end of the barn. The guy was doing a great job so far. The worst duties on the ranch always fell to the new hire, and so far, the short, wiry cowboy was working hard, humming a country tune Holt recognized. Holt was trying to pretend he was doing something else besides assessing the guy, so it was a good thing his father had come along.

"And what's that?" Holt asked his dad.

"What you need," Neal said, pointing a finger at him, "is a *wife*. And not just any wife. One who'll make a good mother for Robby. Someone like the librarian with the curly red hair. Every time your mother and I take Robby to the library and anyone is noisy, she cuts them a look with a serious shush and then there's blessed quiet."

Holt knew the shusher. There was a reason she didn't often work the children's section. Holt once overheard her nastily chastising a woman for putting a book back in the wrong place, and Holt walked up to the mean shusher and pointed at the large framed sign on the wall that read *Choose Kindness*. The shusher turned red, and the chastised woman grinned. "Robby needs a loving mother above all. Someone who can be firm when need be, yes. But loving is number one."

"Well, Charlotte—that's her name—seems like a perfectly good candidate, and I took the liberty of telling her that I have a son who has a young child and maybe she'd like to join us for dinner some time."

Oh God. "Dad, tell me you didn't try to set me up on a date, especially with that woman."

"I sure as hell did. And guess what she said. She said, 'Oh, do you mean Holt? I know him and Robby. They come in every week. I'd love to get to know Holt better.' That means she can handle a boy like Robby."

A boy like Robby. And "direction" from someone like the redhead meant punishment not guidance.

Holt barely held his tongue. He wasn't interested in rehashing Robby's needs with his father. Besides, they'd had this conversation countless times over the past year. "Dad, there's one thing I agree with you on—I do need a good mother for Robby. But she'll be of my choosing. I don't need help in that department."

His father had perked up the moment Holt had said he did need a wife. "Well, your mother and I got hopeful about Amanda, but you two don't seem to be dating."

Maybe we will be. If things went his way. "I'm trying," Holt said. "We'll see."

His father tilted his head. "Ah, well in that case, I'll let you be and stop playing matchmaker. We like Amanda. And Robby clearly does too."

Holt smiled. "He certainly does. She's the whole package, as they say. Everything in one." She really was. Not only was Amanda Jenkins warm and compassionate and patient, but she was funny and charming and interesting and smart. Plus she was beautiful.

"Don't mess it up," Neal Dalton said.

Holt froze, then his skin got itchy, anger swirling in his gut. "Thanks for the vote of confidence."

"Just saying, Holt. Things didn't work out between you two once. Don't let her slip away again."

Out of the mouths of interfering fathers.

His phone pinged with a text. Amanda. How about we have that date tonight?

His heart soared. Perfect, he texted back. Robby is sleeping over in the main house tonight with Dale and Shep. They're having a camp-out in the backyard.

Pick me up at seven?

See you then.

Well. That she'd said they'd talk Monday and she hadn't been able to wait was a very good sign. *No, Dad, I'm not going to mess this up.*

Holt parked in the underground garage for Amanda's building, which sure was swanky. Lots of young men and women were around, coming and going to the pool. In the lobby he buzzed Amanda's apartment, and she told him to come on up.

When she opened the door, his knees almost gave out. He'd never seen her look like this. Ever. She wore a short sleeveless black dress and high-heeled sandals, her long hair loose past her shoulders. Her lips were a sexy red. And the hint of perfume around her was so scintillating it drew him closer.

He could not take his eyes off her and didn't want to. "You look stunning."

"My roommate's the expert on dressing up to go out. She helped me. Shook her head at all my choices for an outfit."

"Well, you'd look stunning in a burlap sack with tomato sauce on your head. But, wow, Amanda."

She laughed. "That may be one of the nicest— and strangest—things anyone's ever said to me."

He'd dressed up too. His brother Morgan had dragged him shopping after they'd moved to Bronco, shaking his own head at how Holt would wear a western shirt and jeans and his *good* cowboy boots to a nice restaurant on a date. Holt was all about cowboy clothes, but apparently, there was an unwritten dress code in fancy Bronco Heights. As he'd driven to Amanda's building, watching the guys walking around, particularly the ones carrying bouquets of flowers for their ladyloves on a Saturday night, he saw how right Morgan was. No one was wearing ranch gear in town tonight.

"You clean up real nice yourself," she said. "Well, let me grab my purse and say goodbye to Poindexter and we'll be off."

Holt glanced past Amanda to the cat sitting on the back of the sofa, grooming his face with a paw. He watched Amanda give the cat a little pat, and then she was back, smelling so delicious he wanted to just wrap himself around her.

He was so aware of her during the walk to the restaurant. Tonight held so many possibilities— for them, for their future and for Robby. Bronco had a couple of nice restaurants, and though he'd love nothing more than to sit down to a plate of DJ's Deluxe's finest ribs, he had something a lot more romantic in mind. There was a small Italian restaurant, low lit, with frescoes on the walls and candelabras. He'd made a reservation, leaving nothing to chance.

Amanda smiled as he led her inside. "I love this place. I've never been here before."

Perfect. A first for them both. They were seated at a round table by a window overlooking the side garden. As he looked at his date across the candlelight, he was taken back to ten years before, when they'd gone to a pizza place and he'd sat across from her so in love, unable to take his eyes off her then too, unable to believe she was his.

"I'm so glad you changed your mind about waiting to respond till Monday," he said. "I don't know how I would have made it through the weekend, not sure what you'd say."

She glanced up from the menu, surprise in her brown eyes. "I like how straightforward you are. You say what's on your mind."

"I've learned my lesson." He nodded.

Crud. Maybe that was the wrong thing to say. The wrong word to mention. She'd said many times that she'd learned her lesson about him, and he certainly didn't want to remind her.

She closed her menu and set it aside and so did he. A waiter took their drink and entrée orders.

"So tell me what brought you to Bronco," he asked. "I don't think we ever talked about that."

She took a sip of her water. "Well, after I got stood up by the man I was about to marry in Vegas, I found myself driving back home and realizing I needed a fresh start. I had a good friend from college who lived in Bronco and had heard such great things about living here, so off I went."

"I'm very sorry you got hurt by that dope in

Vegas, Amanda. But I'm not sorry that it made you available to be sitting right here with me."

"I always go back and forth about fate," she said. "Is this date, this reunion, meant to be? Or did circumstances just put us in the same place at the same time and so here we are?"

The waiter brought their wine and set a basket of Italian bread and a little dish of herb-infused olive oil between them.

"I think it's both," Holt said. "Half fate, half circumstances."

She laughed and lifted her glass. "I will toast to that."

They clinked glasses, the evening off to a great start. They weren't making awkward small talk. This date was about the past, the now and the future.

They talked so easily, Holt telling funny stories about his brothers, more serious ones about his mother's days of recuperation, and his favorite animals on the ranch. And Amanda told him about her clients, including a matchmaker whose success stories included two lonely seventy-somethings who'd recently gotten married and were honeymooning in Italy.

When their entrees came—chicken saltimbocca for him, spaghetti Bolognese for her—they shared bites, talking, laughing, eating, drinking. This evening could not be more perfect—

"Omigod! Holt?"

He glanced up at his name—at that voice— and he did a double take.

Sally Anne.

"Boy, did I surprise you!" Sally Anne said, looking a bit nervous. Then she slid her gaze to Amanda and held out her hand, her long red nails still her trademark, he saw. "I'm Sally Anne— the ex-wife. I'm sure you've heard all about me." She looked back to Holt. "I'm just in town real quick to help out an old friend or otherwise I'd have called."

"So," he said through gritted teeth. "You came to Bronco and didn't even call me to make arrangements to see Robby for even a half hour? You certainly had time to come here, Sally Anne. What the hell?"

"God, Holt. You haven't changed a damned bit. I just don't think I'll have time. My friend is in a bad way, okay? I'm here to pick up dinner for her and I'm leaving early tomorrow morning."

"Do you even care that you have a child?" he asked, red-hot anger pulsating in every part of him.

"I do, of course, I do, Holt. But sometimes

people are just who they damned are. I'm sorry. Just tell Robby I'm sorry."

She ran out of the restaurant.

Holt almost slammed his fist down on the table. "I hate knowing that she was here, right here in town and didn't even plan to see Robby. I hate it. And I hate that you had to witness all that, Amanda."

"Hey, it's okay."

He forced himself to calm down, to suck in a deep breath. It was a good thing they'd almost finished their meals because his appetite was gone, and from the way she pushed her plate away so was hers.

Of all the bad luck of running into her. If only his ex had picked somewhere else to order a meal to go, he never would have known she was in town. He never would have been reminded that she didn't give a rat's butt about her own child.

As Robby's sweet, precious face appeared in his mind, anguish mixed with the anger.

"Let's go, Holt. I'll drive."

He nodded, tossing cash on the table, enough to add a good tip. He needed to get out of here. And he could barely think straight, let alone drive to the ranch.

She didn't say a word on the ride over, didn't ask him questions or make small talk or try to lighten things up. She let him process and digest, which was what he needed.

When she pulled up to the drive at his house, he just sat there like a stone, and she left the engine idling. Maybe he should just send her home and deal with this Sally Anne debacle on his own, in his own way. Whatever the hell *that* meant.

But he needed to get out of the truck, he needed to gulp in some air. And he needed Amanda. He knew it with a certainty that made his chest tight.

What would happen when they went inside, he had no idea. Because he was in a bad place right now. And maybe being with Amanda in the middle of it was going to cost them both.

Chapter Thirteen

Sally Anne sure wasn't what Amanda had expected, not that she'd known what to expect. She really hadn't thought much about Holt's ex; Sally Anne had been just a concept, really, because she wasn't a part of his or Robby's life at all.

But there the woman had been at the tail end of her dinner with Holt. All Amanda wanted was a child and here was Holt's ex-wife, with absolutely no interest in the seven-year-old one she had. Amanda had no idea how that was possible.

The woman had driven away to a new life that didn't include her son. And it had been years.

Then she came to the very town where Holt and Robby lived and hadn't planned to spend any time with her son. That had floored Holt and it had stunned Amanda.

She glanced over at him, the idling engine making the only sound. "Listen Holt, if you need to just be alone right now, I can take the truck home and one of your brothers can bring you by to pick it up tomorrow morning. I'll totally understand if you just need some space."

He turned slightly to her, reaching for her hand and holding it. She liked the connection, that he wasn't shutting her out.

"I could use some coffee," he said. "How about you?"

She gave him a soft smile. "The entire pot, maybe."

She shut off the engine and they went inside, Bentley greeting them. Holt let out the dog, and they sat on the porch and watched Bentley sniff the grass and enjoy the beautiful summer evening weather, then they all headed back in.

She insisted on making the coffee, aware she was too comfortable in his kitchen, and then joined him on the couch, the mugs and a small plate of cookies on the coffee table.

He took a long slug of his coffee, then another,

and turned to her. "Do you get it? Because if you do, can you explain it to me?"

"Are you talking about how Robby's mother can have no interest in his life?" she asked.

He nodded slowly. "How? How is it possible? From the moment I knew he existed I loved him. And that feeling only intensified when the doctor placed him in my arms in the hospital. I love my son with everything I am. How can a parent not feel that way?"

She took a sip of her coffee. "I don't get it either, Holt. All I know is that some people are wired differently. You said Sally Anne left for good when Robby was three. How was she before that?"

"As expected. She didn't want to be a mother. She'd always said that."

"I'm so sorry for all you went through. And I'm so glad Robby had you. Sounds like you more than made up for what he was lacking in his other parent."

He leaned back, and she could almost see the heavy weight pressing on his shoulders. How she wanted to lift it. "A mom, a mom's love and devotion—I want him to have that too."

"I understand," she said, reaching for his hand.

He held it and turned to her again, touching her face. "I'm sorry she ruined our date."

"It's not ruined. In fact, she ended up bringing us closer. I mean, here we are, talking about some very personal issues. You opened up to me, and for that I'm glad."

"I just wish I could shake it," he said. "Just blink that run-in away. But all I see is Robby's face. I hear him asking why his mother isn't in his life."

She wished she knew what to say, but there really wasn't anything to say. She could just be here and hopefully that would help.

He arched one shoulder and grimaced, and she knew his muscles were likely very tight.

"Here, let me," she said, scooting closer and putting her hands on his shoulders. "I remember you always appreciated my back massages at camp after working in the kitchen all day."

She rubbed and kneaded, the soapy masculine scent of him intoxicating. "You can take off your shirt, if you'd like more pressure."

He didn't hesitate. The shirt came off, tossed on the arm of the sofa.

Her hands moved on his bare, broad shoulders. He let out little grunts and ahs, and she could feel him relaxing under her touch.

He turned around, and for a moment, she was dumbstruck by his naked chest. "I want to kiss you," he whispered. "I *need* to kiss you."

There would be no turning back from this point. If they kissed, the kind of kiss she knew it would be—and very likely where it would lead—she'd be all in. Her heart would be his again.

Careful, a little voice said. He got the wind knocked out of him tonight, his faith in people, in the very concept of love was shaken hard; that she knew and understood. Maybe what he wanted and needed was less about her and more about *forgetting* the hard stuff, the hard truths. For tonight.

Then again, she thought, that was life. Stuff happened, and it could bring people closer or pull them apart. *Don't let this pull you and Holt apart when it has nothing to do with you or him—not really. This was about his ex's choices.*

Yes. That was very true.

So maybe she should just go with this. Both fate and circumstances had intervened tonight. So perhaps they should see this to where the evening had led it. Which was a proposed kiss. And, she knew, much more, in his bed. Maybe Holt did need to forget, if just for a little while, the pain deep in his chest, the truth in his head. She could understand that.

Timing is rarely right anyway so don't make it about that.

She leaned close and so did he and he kissed her, deeply. She remembered how she'd once felt about the way he kissed her—as if anything was possible.

"Maybe we shouldn't do this," he said, taking his hand off her back and moving a bit away from her on couch. "I know you wanted to move slowly, Amanda. And suddenly, instead of a candlelit table and a good-night kiss at your door, we're…in dangerous territory. Because I'm using everything I've got to tamp down how badly I want you right now."

There. This wasn't just about him needing to forget what happened earlier.

She stood up and took his hand. He looked at her, holding her gaze so intensely that her knees felt shaky, and she answered by leading the way down the hall and to his bedroom.

"You sure about this?" he asked, staring at her as they entered his bedroom.

She pushed the door closed. "Very." And this time, *she* kissed him, and he responded instantly, taking her face in both of his hands and kissing her so intensely that her knees really did almost buckle.

He turned her around and slowly unzipped the little black dress, then turned her back around and gave it a nudge on each side of her shoulders so that it would fall and slide past her hips onto the floor. She stepped out of it and kicked it aside.

She kissed his bare, muscled chest, which was even sexier than she'd remembered. He picked her up and carried her onto the bed, getting rid of his pants, and slowly taking off her lacy bra. His hands and mouth were all over her, exploring, enjoying, savoring. For the first time in a long time she didn't think; she just *felt*. And apparently, the same went for him.

Her eyes closed, she felt her lacy undies being pulled down and removed. She arched her back and kissed him, anticipating the feel of him on top of her. She opened her eyes, and he was reaching for his bedside table, opening a drawer. She watched him rip open the foil packet and then met his gaze as he leaned over her.

"To a fresh start," she whispered. "To the future."

"I will make love to that," he said.

And then every painful memory from the past and every new worry was replaced by pure sensation.

The faint sound of roosters crowing woke Holt at rancher's hours: before the crack of dawn. He glanced to the left, and there was Amanda, beautiful, sexy, loving Amanda, sleeping, her face turned away from him, her long dark hair down one shoulder.

To a fresh start...to the future.

Her words echoing in his head, Holt turned away, a chill creeping up his spine. Last night, those words had sounded so good. But suddenly...

Suddenly what? Why did he feel like bolting out of bed and making himself scarce?

Fight against it, he told himself. *You're just letting your old fears get to you. That this isn't going to work out. That you're not ever going to be enough for her.*

But something else was poking at him too. Something that said: *It's Robby who's going to get hurt when she leaves you. You'll disappoint her, Robby will be too much, more than she realized, and suddenly, your heart is handed back to you and your son is sobbing.*

Oh hell. That tightness in his chest was back, and he stared up at the ceiling. Last night was everything he remembered and so much more. He and Amanda had been perfect fits, in sync, in harmony, and he'd released what felt like years of pent-up frustration. All he'd kept thinking—when he'd been able to process thought—was that he had Amanda back, and everything in his world had felt right again.

But the weight of that world was now back, pressing down hard. He tried to keep it at bay, to just keep thinking about what he wanted for

Robby, but he couldn't stop all the echoes in his head. People, even those closest to you—*I'm talking about you, Dad*—couldn't be trusted. People walked out. *That's you, Sally Anne*. People disappointed. *That's me*.

Why had he thought he and Amanda could have a second chance, that they could find what they needed in each other? He'd believed he was thinking about his son's needs when he'd proposed they try again. But hadn't everything they'd been through hammered home that the fairy tale he sought for Robby didn't exist?

He wasn't letting anyone in to hurt Robby again, to turn Holt's life upside down. They had a good thing going here at Dalton's Grange. They had family, even with his issues with his dad. He had nothing to prove to his father anymore and hell if he'd make Robby prove anything to his grandfather. Right now, Robby was over at the main house, having a sleepover in the backyard with Shep and Dale. Between his grandmother and his uncles and Holt, Robby had all the love and support he needed. Holt wasn't going to let anyone come in and break his son's heart by leaving.

He could feel himself getting farther and farther away from thinking he and Amanda could have a shot, that their relationship would work out, that she would still find Robby so lovable after a few weeks.

Damn, you're cynical, he thought. Yeah, but how could he not be? There was Sally Anne's appearance and the sickening truth that she didn't care about Robby. And now there was Holt's disillusionment all over again when he'd just been building his faith in life and love back up.

What the hell was the point?

He felt Amanda stir beside him. And everything inside him went cold and hard, like stone. Now he was going to hurt her when she didn't deserve it. *He'd* brought up the second chance. *He'd* brought up the idea of them fulfilling each other's needs and hopes and dreams. She'd been saying all along that she didn't want to go back, that she couldn't.

And he'd brought her right in.

He wasn't too fond of himself at the moment.

Holt had thought he'd been taking his father's advice—his father's good advice—to not mess things up with Amanda. All Holt *had* done was mess up. Bad.

His phone rang, and Holt grabbed it off his bedside table. His dad. Calling at 5:52 a.m.?

He bolted upright. Had something happened to Robby?

Amanda sat up too, looking at him in with concern as she pulled the quilt up to cover herself.

"You'd better come get your son," Neal Dalton said—grumpily. "He woke up too early and is bouncing off the walls."

He shook his head. "Seriously, Dad."

"Oh, I'm being serious, all right," Neal said. "Robby took it upon himself to make his grandmother and me coffee and managed to break not only the carafe but a mug. It's just too much, Holt, and I want you to come get him right now."

"Look," Holt said. "I get that he broke something. But you can't just clean it up and ask him to be more careful? He thought he was doing something nice for you and Mom."

"Just come get him."

Holt hung up.

"Dammit," he said, reaching for his boxer briefs, which he quickly put on as surreptitiously as possible.

"What's going on?" Amanda asked.

He stalked to his dresser and pulled on jeans and a T-shirt. "I'm sorry, Amanda. But I've got to go get Robby. He woke up too early and is already breaking things by accident and driving my dad nuts. Why don't you take my truck home, and I'll have one of my brothers drive me over to get it later. You can leave the keys in the console."

She hesitated a second before saying, "Okay." Then another pause.

He didn't know how he'd expected this morning to go, but leaving her to drive herself home while he left wasn't it. The idea of that made him feel like hell, but having her here this early when he walked back in with Robby would be kind of awkward too.

He let out a breath and turned to look at her. "I'm sorry I'm being so abrupt. I woke up feeling kind of…unsettled, and then the phone rang and made it worse."

"Unsettled?" she asked, pulling on her clothes. Her movements were so fast and stiff, and he knew he'd made her feel off balance. All he wanted to do was take her in his arms and just hold her—not say anything because he had no idea what he wanted to say. But he had to go. And he needed the space to think anyway.

"Can we talk later, Amanda? I mean, really talk."

She stared at him for a second and then finally nodded.

He wasn't even sure what he planned to say.

Chapter Fourteen

Amanda very quietly entered her apartment, not wanting to wake up Brittany or be caught slinking in like this in last night's clothes. Brittany would want details, and Amanda would burst into tears. She'd been trying not to cry since she'd left Dalton's Grange—in Holt's truck.

Poindexter padded over for some attention, so she picked him up and nuzzled him, giving him a few good scratches along his back, then fed him breakfast. She could use coffee, but what she really needed was a hot, bracing shower.

It was under the water, washing away all traces

of last night, washing away Holt's scent, that she let herself give into how she was feeling—and she cried. Hard. Something had shifted deep within her. The way he'd let her inside, opened up to her, after such a tumultuous, emotional incident, had made her feel so close to him. And as she'd fallen asleep after they'd made love, she'd truly thought they were a united team, that they'd found their way to each other. Her heart had opened to him. Fully.

And this morning, she'd felt him close his own.

In her bathrobe, her hair damp down her back, she could swear she smelled coffee brewing, the chocolate-hazelnut roast she loved. Which meant that Brittany was awake. Thank God. Now that Amanda had gotten the crying out of her system, she could use some Brittany wisdom.

As she walked into the kitchen, her roommate, looking gorgeous as usual even though she'd just rolled out of bed, was studying her.

"So, I heard the door open and close a little while ago," Brittany said, her dark eyes shrewd. "Then I heard the shower start. That tells me a few things. But I hope I've got it wrong."

Amanda bit her lip. "You don't, I'm sure."

Brittany poured them each a mug of coffee and brought the creamer and sugar to the table. "That you didn't come home last night means the night started out great. That you didn't come home till 6:00 a.m. means the night *ended* great. But that you're home this early and taking a shower here means something went wrong this morning."

"Are you sure you're not clairvoyant?" Amanda asked, smiling for the first time since she woke up.

Brittany took a sip of her coffee. "Oh, just been there, experienced that. But I'm usually the one making something go wrong and leaving."

Maybe that was the way. Because then, you didn't get hurt. But Holt had seemed as conflicted as Amanda was. "Everything was going great and then disaster struck. More like a tornado. We were having an amazing time together at that little Italian place at the end of Main Street," Amanda said, thinking back to the restaurant, so romantic, the candlelit table, the delicious food, the good wine. "And toward the end of dinner, guess who suddenly appeared out of nowhere, picking up takeout. Holt's ex-wife."

Brittany raised an eyebrow. "The one who hasn't been around in a few years? Why was she here? To spend time with her son?"

"An old friend was having problems, apparently. She wasn't even planning on seeing Robby. I don't get it. Neither does Holt. They had words about that, and he was so upset about his ex's complete lack of regard for their child that I drove him home. Then we got to talking about it and one thing led to another and…we were in bed."

"Tell me that part was good," Brittany said with a gentle smile.

"Amazing. Beautiful. Everything I remember and everything I imagined being with him again would be like. I'm so damned in love with the guy, Brittany."

"I know," her roommate said, squeezing her hand. "So all the negative energy from the ex got pushed aside for something much better at his place last night, but then it all came back to him this morning?"

Amanda tilted her head. "You know, I didn't really think about it like that, but yeah, I guess it must have. He said he felt unsettled, and I'm sure that was why. And maybe both parts of his past coming at him." She sipped her coffee, wishing she understood better. "The ex-wife. The ex-girlfriend."

"So what caused you to come home?"

"His son had slept over at his grandparents and Holt got call to come get him. Robby was either too loud or broke something or both."

"Ah. The triple whammy. The ex-wife infuriating him. The hopeful second chance with the woman he never forgot. And his grumpy father, impatient with his son. All in one brief period of time. Enough to rattle the calmest of us."

That made her feel better for herself—and terrible for Holt. "You think so?"

"The ex-wife's appearance would be enough, Amanda. From everything you've said, Holt's a really devoted dad. His son is the world to him. And the boy's mother comes to town and doesn't even arrange to see her own kid?" She shook head. "Holt's probably just all tangled up. Wishing things could be different and knowing they can't be."

"Well, maybe he thinks *we* can't be either," Amanda said. "He just seemed so defeated this morning."

"Give him a little time. I have faith," Brittany said.

Amanda sighed. "Wish I did." Maybe she would if she hadn't been dumped by Holt once already.

"I know he picked you up last night, so you drove his car home this morning?"

Amanda nodded, then got up and headed for the fridge, needing some sourdough toast with butter and jam, pure comfort breakfast. "Want some?" she asked Brittany, holding up the sourdough bread.

"Sure do," Brittany said with a smile. "Well,

then he'll come by some time this morning to pick up the car. You'll talk then. And be smooching a big hot hello."

Amanda laughed, then her smile faded. "He told me to just leave the keys in the truck's console, so he doesn't even have to come up for them."

"Trust me, he'll come up."

Amanda hoped so. Or she'd go out of her mind wondering what was going on with them, what he was thinking. She didn't want to be shut out. Not when they'd both let each other *in*.

After breakfast, when Brittany left to take her own shower, Amanda headed over to her laptop on the coffee table and checked her email—and almost jumped.

There was a response to her last post on the group chat site about adoptees seeking information on their birth parents. Amanda hadn't had much information to share on the site, just the general birth year, possible birth place, which might not even be accurate, and the birth parents' names— she kept it surnames only for privacy—but she'd hoped that would be enough to connect with someone out there. And for Josiah Abernathy and Winona Cobbs to be reunited with the baby girl they'd had to give up—the baby girl Winona had been told had died.

Amanda clicked on the email.

Hi. My name is Bernadette Jefferson and I was born in Rust Creek Falls and placed for adoption with a loving family. When my parents passed on, I found a document in their keepsake trunk with the name Abernathy—it was with my birth certificate. Abernathy isn't a very common name so I think I might be who you're looking for. I know my birth parents would be very elderly if still alive. This is the first time I've had hope so thank you for that! Please be in touch at your earliest convenience.

With hope, Bernadette Jefferson

Amanda burst out of her chair, scooped up Poindexter and danced him around the living room. "Poin! I think we found the long-lost baby daughter of Winona Cobbs and Josiah Abernathy! After seventy-five years!"

Poindexter did not seem to care, but he liked being held so he went with the dance.

"Ooh, I have to text Mel right away!" She put down the cat and ran for her phone. It was six thirty, but she *had* to tell Mel this great news right away, even if it meant the notification would awaken her and possibly Gabe if she was at his ranch this morning. Amanda knew her friend would want to know about the response right away. Especially because it was so promising. Abernathy *wasn't* a common name. And the timing and birth place matched!

She copied and pasted the email into a text and sent it to Mel. Five seconds later, her phone pinged back.

Omigosh! Mel texted. You're amazing—thank you so much for helping us! This is our first real lead and it sounds so promising! I'll respond to her. Thanks again, Amanda!

The email and Mel's response had done wonders for Amanda's battered spirit.

The half-mile walk to the main house had done little to clear Holt's head. The way he'd treated Amanda… He'd reached for his phone three times to at least text her an *I'm sorry*, then put it back in his pocket. He had to break the urge to connect with her. The yearning for her. He had to let her go.

He'd taken Bentley with him, letting the dog walk along unleashed at his side. In the distance he could see Robby kicking a soccer ball, his grandmother sitting on the wraparound porch, cheering him on. Neal Dalton was nowhere to be found.

"Bentley!" Robby shouted, and came running, the border collie sprinting toward him. Robby dropped to his knees, hugging and kissing his beloved dog, the boy rolling on the grass and Bentley following suit.

This was what childhood was supposed to be, Holt thought. Exactly this. *And* making mistakes. And accepting the consequences for them. But those consequences right now included a grumpy, impatient grandfather. Holt had always thought Robby and Neal Dalton would have to meet each other halfway—Robby being more mindful, particularly when he was around his grandfather, and Neal being more patient and understanding that his grandson had a harder time controlling his impulses than some other kids.

If your father can't change, Holt's mother had said once, *I don't know why he expects a little boy to be able to change.*

Holt had appreciated that then, that his mother understood. But in the year Holt and Robby had been just a half mile away, the boy spending a lot of time with his grandparents, Neal Dalton hadn't become more accepting of his grandson.

As Holt got closer, Robby catapulted himself into his father's arms, and Holt lifted his boy up and held him tight. He loved this child with all his heart. *Everything* was right here.

His mother waved with a big smile and went inside, then came back out with a bowl of what looked like water, Holt's dad behind her. She set the bowl down by the door—for Bentley, he realized with a smile—then called Robby into the house for lemonade and a muffin. Thank God for his mother. She was the one who'd asked Holt to rethink his *no* about working for his father, living on Dalton's Grange, and he'd say yes all over again for his mother's sake. But it was time for him and his dad to come to terms about the way he responded to Robby. Given his father's expression right now, which was along the lines of I've-had-it-up-to-here and Holt's matching thought, he had no idea how this conversation would go.

Look, Robby's teacher had said when Holt had been honest about his dad's impatience with Robby at home. *That's part of the consequences of Robby's behavior. And part of your job is helping Robby manage that—from dealing with people's negative reactions to his behavior, from strangers to classmates and staff, to family. It's all valid, Holt.*

"Finally," Neal Dalton said as Holt got closer.

Holt glared at his dad. Sometimes, he'd see his father in front of the grand, majestic mansion and he'd try to reconcile the man he'd always known with this new rich Neal Dalton who owned this

beautiful home and all this land. This successful ranch. His father had changed—because his
wife's health scare and a big pile of money had
given him a second chance.

It's what you do with what you have, Holt
thought as his father came down the stairs.

*So why the hell can't I apply that way of think-
ing to me and Amanda? Why am I so sure it'll
all fall apart?*

Because it always does, he reminded himself,
thinking of Sally Anne.

His mother came back out with a doggie bis-
cuit, which she set on the cushy mat in front of
Bentley, who was enjoying the shade. She gave
the dog a pat.

"If you can't be more patient with Robby, then
I don't think you should be around him, Dad. He
needs people on his side. Yes, he needs guidance
and correction—from me, his parent—not you.
Do I make myself clear?"

His father seemed taken aback. "How dare you
talk to me like that!"

"I dare because I have to."

Neal Dalton shook his head. "Trust me, Holt.
You were the same way as Robby at his age and
I said the same nonsense—oh, he'll grow out of
it. And look what happened when you got older.
Making trouble, getting arrested for nonsense.

Running wild. Marrying a woman who doesn't even care about her own child."

Holt winced, feeling like a left hook had just landed in his stomach. What the hell?

"You're done telling me who I am or who I was. I'm proud of the man I've become. And I'm damned proud of the father I am." He glanced behind his father to the house. "Robby!" he shouted. "Come on out, buddy. Time to go."

"'Kay, Daddy!" Robby shouted back, racing out the door and down the steps, half a muffin in his hand. It was clear from his tone that Robby hadn't heard any of what his grandfather had said. "Come on, Bentley. Race ya home!"

Robby and the dog went flying up the path.

"When Robby breaks his leg and lands face-first in that muffin in his hand," his father said, "don't cry to me."

Holt shook his head and turned to his mother. "Mom, if you'd like to see me or Robby, it'll have to be at my place. I love you but I'm done here." He hugged his mother, glared at his father and then turned and walked toward home, his heart heavier than it was when he'd left his house, and that was saying something.

On Monday afternoon Amanda arrived at Holt's house for the tutoring session with Robby, not sure he'd even open the door. But he did. He hadn't called or texted since yesterday morning when she'd left his bed. She'd thought for sure he wouldn't let the day pass without at least a text, just something, but not a word.

He stood in the doorway, looking both gorgeous and miserable.

"I'm here to tutor Robby," she said, lifting her chin. She wasn't going to let her issues with Holt stop her from keeping her commitment to help Robby with reading.

"I know I said we'd talk. And I want to, Amanda. Can you stay after?"

She nodded, and because she knew him better than she thought, she could tell he was relieved— that she was here, that she actually wanted to talk to him at all. Then again, *he* probably just wanted closure on this—to end their budding second chance.

She'd never felt so…up in the air. Before—with Holt, with Tyler and his hellish text right before their wedding—she'd had no doubt where she stood: a big fat nowhere. Things had been over, kaput. Now? This? She didn't know. And that was bad too. Hell yeah, they'd talk after.

Upstairs, she found Robby preparing for their tutoring session as he always did, taking his favorite books from his bookshelf and making a pile. Bentley was on his bed and Oliver was on his perch.

"Hey, Robby!" Amanda said.

He ran over for a hug, talking a mile a minute about his camp-out sleepover with his uncles at the main house, how they'd made s'mores and Shep had brought out his telescope and he saw the Big Dipper and a zillion stars and maybe even planets.

"But then I broke stuff in the kitchen and Gramps yelled at me," he said, tears welling in his big blue eyes. "He told me I never learn and he'd had it." He looked at Amanda, biting his lip. "Do you think that means he doesn't want to be my granddaddy anymore?"

Amanda felt her eyes sting with tears. She sat down on Robby's bed and patted the space beside her. He came and sat down, wiping under his eyes.

"Did you talk to your dad about this?" Amanda asked.

Robby nodded. "He said that my gramps will always be my gramps no matter what and that he loves me very much. And Daddy also said that Gramps needed more patience and that I needed to be more careful. But I tried to be, I really did. I just wanted to make my gram and gramps coffee."

Amanda put her arm around him. "I know,

sweetheart. And that was very thoughtful of you. I'm sorry it didn't work out the way you wanted. Maybe next time you want to do something like that, you could ask for a grown-up's help, like one of your uncles. That way, if anything breaks, *they'll* get in trouble and not you." She gave Robby an evil grin.

Robby laughed. "Hey, yeah, that's a really good idea. My dad is always saying I should think hard first before I decide to do something. And next time I'll think to ask someone for help." He nodded, brightening so much that Amanda's heart moved in her chest.

Oh, how she loved this boy.

"I picked out two books to read. Did you know that Rocco the Raccoon loves spinach? I tried it cuz of that and it wasn't as terrible as I thought it would be. Not like broccoli." He scrunched up his face. "I hate broccoli."

"I *looove* broccoli!" she said. "I can't wait to hear the Rocco story about spinach."

Robby grabbed the book and settled onto the floor on top of his round reading rug, white and blue with silver stars and lots of floor pillows. Bentley jumped down and curled up beside him. Oliver watched from his perch, then closed his eyes again.

As Robby sat beside her, tongue out in concentration, finger moving under the words, Amanda knew she wasn't giving up on this family. She loved both father and son with everything she was.

She'd give Holt his chance to say what he wanted to say. And then she'd make some decisions. Hard ones.

Chapter Fifteen

Turned out that the two youngest Dalton brothers, Shep and Dale, who lived in the main house, had filled in Morgan and Boone on what had happened with Robby that morning, so the four Daltons insisted on taking Robby to town for cheer-up burgers, fries and ice cream after his tutoring session. Another major plus in the working-for-his-dad column was that Holt and his brothers had gotten closer, and they all adored Robby. They also knew what a hothead their father could be.

Now, a few minutes after Robby had gone off with his uncles, Holt and Amanda sat across from each other at the kitchen table, a mug of coffee in front of each, neither saying a word. Amanda sipped her coffee. Holt stared out the window at the moment, trying to figure out where to start, what to say. How to do the least damage.

Amanda cleared her throat. "Before we started reading, Robby told me what happened at the main house this morning. He asked me if his grandfather didn't love him anymore."

Holt winced, but before he could respond, Amanda continued.

"I did my best to tell him that his grandfather *does* love him," she said. "As he told me you did. But it got me thinking, Holt. That's how I'm left feeling right now. Unsure of where I stand. Off balance. Last night, in your bed, in your arms, all I could think was how much I still love you. How I have you back. And then bam, all I feel is a cold draft."

How much I still love you...

He'd done a double take at those words, staring at her as if shocked she'd said such a thing. He kind of was, though. Shocked. That she felt that way. That she'd said it.

She met his gaze, but when he didn't say anything, she sighed and looked out the window.

He had no idea how he felt. Everything—all

the complex layers of what was going on in his life—was balled up so tight.

Dammit. This was not what he wanted. He'd made Amanda feel the way his father had made Robby feel. The way his father had made *him* feel. How had he screwed up to this degree?

Love was powerful and all-consuming and *everything*. And right now, he needed to reserve it all for Robby. "I thought I had things figured out," he said, staring at his coffee before looking up to face her. "I thought I could do this. But then I realized I can't. I'm not about to let Robby get hurt all over again."

Amanda gasped. "What? You think I'm going to hurt Robby?"

"You won't mean to. You won't want to. But you'll leave and he'll be devastated and think it's his fault. I went through all that with him once and the after-effects are horribly painful and long-lasting. We won't go through that again. I won't allow it."

Amanda stood up. "Are you kidding me? You're ending things between us—when we just got started—because you *expect* me to break both your hearts?"

He got up too, moving to the counter to lean against it. "Yes."

She glared at him, but then her expression softened into something more like sadness. "That's what you think of me? That's how little you trust me?"

"I don't trust anyone," he said. "Except Robby."

She was staring at him, sparks in her eyes. "Holt. This is no way to live. Expecting everyone to be like Sally Anne. Hell, *you* were Sally Anne in our last go around. Not me."

I did the same thing then that I'm doing now, he realized, his heart cracking. He was leaving Amanda before she could leave him. And this time—Robby.

He hated the wall he felt building around the weaker one she'd managed to get past. "I never wanted to hurt you, Amanda. You mean a lot to me. You know that. But I can't do this. I won't do this. I have to protect Robby."

She shook her head. "I know how much you love your son. I understand how you feel, Holt. I know what that run-in with Sally Anne did to you. But you're going to throw love away in case it doesn't work out? Does that really make sense to you?"

"I need to focus on my son, Amanda. There's no room in my life for anyone but him right now." There, he came out and said it, openly and honestly. No miscommunication. "I need to protect

Robby—heart, mind and soul," he added, hoping she understood.

Tears welled her in her eyes.

And I need to protect myself, he said silently.

Holt crossed his arms over his chest. "I'll take over working with him on reading. I'm not an expert, of course, but I did some research on how to help a struggling reader improve."

She barely nodded and headed for the door. "I guess this is goodbye, then." She whirled around. "For the record, though, Holt. I think you're wrong here. I love you and the two of us have something very special. And I love Robby, and he and I have a very special relationship too. Same goes for the three of us. We fit. We blend. We belong together, Holt. I'd lost my ability to believe in love, but my feelings for you and for Robby renewed it. I'm glad I believe—even if it means hurting this bad. And for a long time. Because at least I *feel*. At least I *try*."

She pulled open the door and left, and it took everything in him not to follow her, to keep her talking, keep her in sight. But he had to let her go. For everyone's sake. And that included her own.

"Goldilocks is gonna be okay, right, Daddy?" Robby asked, sitting beside Holt in the small barn where they were nursing one of their ill goats back to health. So far, so good.

For the goat, anyway. Holt was another story. Almost a week had passed since his awful conversation with Amanda. He hadn't called or texted and neither had she. Sometimes he missed her so much he felt sick. And there was no medicine. But spending the past few days with Robby and poor Goldilocks practically 24/7 had done wonders for the ill goat.

"I think she'll be fine," Holt assured his son. "She probably just needs a day or two more of round-the-clock care. Thanks to you, she's on the mend."

Robby beamed. "I did help, didn't I, Daddy?"

Holt nodded, slinging an arm around Robby's shoulders. "You did more than just help. You saved that goat's life. If you hadn't insisted on us sleeping right outside her pen, we might not have been there when she needed us at three in the morning two nights ago. You were right to argue for that." Goldilocks had needed constant fluids, but she'd worsened. Thanks to Robby's sweet insistence on camping outside her pen "just in case," they'd been ready with water when the goat had needed it.

He'd known, of course, that Robby cared about the animals on the ranch, from the cattle to the small number of farm animals like the goats and lambs, but the extent of his compassion and his interest in Goldie's illness had surprised him. Holt also knew that kids whose attention could generally be all over the place could focus intently on things that supremely held their interest. Robby had not only just wanted to sit outside Goldie's pen and monitor her, but he'd done his own research about her illness via a kid's farming website and had learned a lot about goats and illness in the process. A lot of text for a little boy who struggled with reading. But he'd worked hard. Granted, Robby was only seven, but for him to say he wanted to be a "doctor for farm animals" was a big deal.

And Robby looked so proud right now. Goldilocks was a favorite of Holt's mother, and she'd been out helping to care for the goat too. Holt had avoided his dad the past several days, easy to do on the vast ranch. The couple of times he'd seen his dad headed in his direction, Holt turned. And he'd kept Robby away from the main house too. That hadn't felt good at all. But the burn in his gut over his problems with his dad, especially where Robby was concerned, kept his mind off Amanda. Until late at night when he would try to sleep and all he could think about was her.

Their last night together.

How he missed her.

How he wished he could undo hurting her without undoing the part that kept him and Robby on the right track.

"I hear Goldie's better, thanks to you two," a familiar voice said.

Neal Dalton. He was in his work clothes, his jeans and a western shirt with a leather vest, and his black Stetson. He had his phone in his hand, as usual. His sons managed various aspects of the ranch and one of them was always contacting him. Holt had simply avoided checking in with his father about anything that had come up the past bunch of days. He'd just dealt with whatever needed dealing with.

"Gramps, guess what?" Robby said. "I helped mix Goldilocks's yogurt and honey. And she ate most of it!"

One of the pluses of Robby's impulsivity was that he didn't shy away from people who he knew were upset with him. That always helped smooth things over since Robby rarely cowered or ran off. But his grandfather was a tough customer.

Neal Dalton smiled and took off his hat. "I heard that you've taken real good care of her. You saved your gram's favorite goat. I'm proud of you, Robby."

"You are?" Robby asked, tilting his head.

"Sure am," Neal said.

Holt had never been able to read his father all that well, but the different emotions on the man's face clued him in that Neal Dalton was uncomfortable as heck right now. His father seemed about to say something, then clamped his mouth shut, glancing over at Goldie. Neal ran a hand under his right eye, then his left, and Holt peered more closely at him.

Was his father *crying*?

Robby got up, hay in his hair and all over his back. He walked over to his gramps and pulled out a baggie with carrot slices, which they'd packed just in case the goat got well enough to have the special teat. "I walked and didn't run this time. Do you want some carrots, Gramps? Goldilocks isn't feeling good enough to have them yet."

Neal Dalton slashed a quick hand under both eyes again, then wrapped Robby in a hug. "I'd love a carrot, Robby. And thank you for walking and not running."

Robby smiled. "Because sometimes it can make the animals feel scared. I wouldn't want Goldilocks to feel scared."

"I'll bet she really appreciates that you're taking such good care of her," Neal said, his eyes soft.

Robby grinned, glancing at the goat, then his face fell and he looked down at the floor.

"I'm sorry I'm not a good grandson." His eyes welled with tears. "I really am trying to be better, Gramps."

Holt closed his eyes for a second, his own eyes stinging. *Oh, Robby*, he thought, wanting to scoop up his boy and hold him close, save him, somehow, from this hurt.

And if his father blew his response, there'd be hell to pay.

He'd give Neal Dalton five seconds to make this right.

Neal Dalton's face almost crumpled. "You're a great grandson, Robby. Of course you are. I'm so glad you're my grandboy."

Holt almost gasped, his heart squeezing in his chest. Robby's face brightened, the tears abating.

"Now, it is true that sometimes you're a little too loud or fast or wild for me," Neal continued. "But I'm an impatient type. But you know what, Robby? I'm gonna try to be more patient because I love you and I want us to spend more time together. We'll both try."

Robby smiled and seemed about to jump up and down, then thought better of it. "Daddy always says that all we can do is try."

This time, Holt did gasp. As Amanda's words came back to him. *I'm glad I believe—even if it means hurting this bad. And for a long time. Because at least I feel. At least I try.*

He didn't want to think about this right now. Things were finally okay. Yeah, he missed the hell out of Amanda but this—him and Robby, on the ranch, his livelihood and future and Robby's legacy—was how it was supposed to be.

"I am very sorry for making you feel bad, Robby," Neal said. "I shouldn't have because I love you so much."

Robby smiled. "I love you, Gramps." The boy hugged his grandfather tight, Neal Dalton scooping Robby up and holding him close.

Well, *that* was all very unexpected. The relief that came over Holt undid muscles he hadn't even realized were bunch up and stiff. He was about to pull his dad aside and tell him how much all that meant to him when a gruff voice sounded from outside the barn.

"Holt Dalton!" a man called out. "I'm looking for Holt Dalton."

Holt frowned and eyed his dad and shrugged. "Robby, you wait with Goldie, okay?"

"Okay," Robby said, sitting on a stool just outside the pen with his Rocco the Raccoon book. "I'll read to her."

Holt nodded, and then he and his father walked

out. Standing in front of the barn, hands on hips, was Edward Thompson.

A vein was popping in the man's neck, his blue eyes shooting sparks. "My daughter informed me this morning that she and your ranch hand are engaged," Thompson said. "That is absolutely unacceptable, and I want to know how you're going to fix this mess."

Engaged. Holt wasn't surprised to hear that. That meant Brody and Piper had made their plan. "I did talk to Brody," Holt said. "He's a smart, levelheaded young man who loves your daughter very much. In fact, he has Piper's interests above his own. If he proposed, it's because he has a solid plan for their present and their future."

Thompson grimaced. "Oh please. All she is to him is a pretty girl with a rich daddy. Give me a break."

"That's how little respect you have for your daughter?" Neal Dalton asked, staring Edward Thompson down. "That she'd choose a man like that?"

"A *man*? The kid is eighteen," Thompson bellowed. He shook his head. "I guess I'll just have to take away the money I set aside for college. We'll see how fast she runs off with that boy when that part of her plan falls through. Love.

What the hell does either of them think they know about love?" He shook his head again.

"So you'd rather lose your daughter than try to see things through her eyes?" Holt asked. "To understand how she feels?"

"I'm coming down hard on her for her own good!" Thompson said, crossing his arms over his chest.

"No, Thompson," Neal said. "And it's too bad you can't love her for who she is instead of who you want her to be. I almost made that mistake myself with my grandson. And my son. But considering you don't give your daughter any credit…"

Huh. Would wonders never cease. His father was surprising him left and right this morning.

"Don't you tell me how I feel about my daughter!" the man boomed. "I love that girl with all my heart."

"If you did, you'd care how she'd felt," Neal said.

"I care how she feels," Thompson countered. "But she's throwing her life away!"

"Is she?" Neal asked. "Because she fell in love with a terrific young man who's making his own way? I heard you did too, that you started from nothing."

Edward Thompson lifted his chin. "I didn't

work so hard to own a very successful corporation so that my daughter could take up with a ranch hand."

"Interesting point of view," Neal said. "Because I heard a little bit about your family. Your wife, Marianne, eloped with you when you barely had a hundred dollars to your name. And you're happily married to this day."

Thompson seemed to think about that for a moment, but then he frowned. "Marianne was denied a lot for years. And worked hard right beside me. I don't want that for Piper."

"Well, Piper is her own person," Neal countered. "Give yourself some credit for how you raised her. And give her some credit too."

Holt could see the man was relenting. Slowly, but he was.

"Holt here was a ranch hand with nothing to his name at eighteen," Neal continued. "Now, I couldn't be prouder of the man he is." His father turned to him. "You tried to tell me and I wouldn't listen. I called *you* stubborn? No one is more stubborn than I am. Except for maybe Thompson here. I'm sorry, Holt. For everything. I hope you can forgive me."

Once again, Holt almost gasped. He certainly hadn't expected his father to say anything like that. And he could tell Neal Dalton had meant every word.

"You got it, Dad. We'll talk later?"

Neal nodded, then turned to their guest. "Look, Thompson, why don't you come up to the house for some coffee," Neal offered. "We've got a lot in common, more than either of us thought, most likely. Let's talk this through."

Thompson's shoulders slumped. "Guess I could use some caffeine."

And just like that, the two men nodded at Holt and then headed up the path toward the main house. Holt had a feeling his father and Thompson were going to be solid friends. And that Brody and Piper would end up with Edward Thompson's blessing. Maybe not today but very soon.

Holt went back into the barn and smiled at Robby. "How's Goldie doing?"

"She loves this book," Robby said. "I read the whole thing to her. And I only messed up a few times. I wish I could tell Amanda about that but she hasn't been around. How come, Daddy?"

Holt's stomach twisted and he sat back down beside his son, his knees drawn up to his chest. "Well, I decided I wanted to do your reading with you. That way I get to spend even more time with you before school starts. I can't believe the summer is coming to an end so soon."

"I miss Amanda, though, Daddy. She's so nice."

Holt's heart squeezed and he reached a hand over to brush back Robby's ever-present mop of bangs from his eyes. "Yeah, she is."

"Do you miss her too?"

"I do," Holt answered honestly.

"Then you should ask her to come over for lunch, Daddy. You make the best grilled cheese. And then the three of us can take Bentley for a walk in the woods."

"Not today," Holt said. "But I promise you that grilled cheese for lunch. And the walk in the woods."

Robby brightened. "I wish Oliver could come too. And Amanda."

Me, too, Holt thought.

"Daddy, if you and Amanda got into a fight, you just have to become friends again. Did I tell you that I saw Ethan at the burger place when my uncles took me, and Ethan came over and said he was sorry about being mean at the fun run and he asked if I wanted to help him build his new Lego set?"

Holt smiled. "Yup, you told me. And I'm really glad about it."

"Ethan said he didn't know he was being mean when he said those things about my mom."

Holt tilted his head. "What do you think about that?"

"I believe him. I think most kids have moms so they don't understand when someone's mom isn't around."

Holt nodded, again wishing he could protect Robby from this—from the truth. And that was crazy. He couldn't. Helping him deal with the truth, particularly when it reared its ugly head— that was what Holt could do for his son. "Yeah."

"But my mom isn't here and even though sometimes I get sad about it, I like to be happy."

Holt felt the backs of his eyes sting. "I'm so glad you do, Robby. That's a great attitude." It really was.

"You know what? I think people can choose to be grumpyheads like Gramps used to be. Or nice, like Gramps is now. Don't you think, Daddy?"

Holt smiled. "I suppose so. Though I guess sometimes people can't help how they feel."

"I don't know about that. Uncle Morgan said you can't make other people do what you want, but you can make yourself do what you want. I'm saying it wrong, but I think I knew what he meant."

So did Holt. That you couldn't control others, but you could control your reactions to them.

How did a seven-year-old get to be so wise?

Robby had this wonderful ability to take in the best parts, the positive parts, of chaos around him.

"Like Ethan," Robby continued. "He couldn't make me want to be friends with him after he was mean to me so he said sorry. And now we're friends."

On the very edges of Holt's consciousness, he knew there was a lesson in there for him, but the new wall he'd erected around himself was impenetrable. He'd made it that way.

"I'm gonna read Goldilocks another book about Rocco," Robby said. "You can listen too, Daddy."

"I will," he said, wanting to grab his son and hold him tight and never let him go. But also on the edges of that consciousness he knew he had to do just that. He had to have faith in his smart, caring, wonderful son to fight his own battles, work out his issues. Even at seven years old.

And Holt, at thirty-two, had to do the same. Damned if he knew how right now, though. Because when he thought about it, Holt had knocked *himself* out.

Chapter Sixteen

"Hi, Daring Drake!" a familiar little voice said as footsteps bounded. "I'm back to see you! How are you? How's life?"

Amanda's heart quickened as she rounded the "Adoptable Animals" barn at Happy Hearts Animal Sanctuary, expecting to see Robby Dalton any second since that was definitely his voice she'd heard. And yup, there he was, in an orange T-shirt and khaki shorts, standing pressed against the wooden fence where the dear old cows were grazing in their pasture.

Amanda braced herself to come face-to-face

with Holt, but she looked around and didn't see him anywhere. An entire week had gone by since she *had* seen him, the night he'd broken her heart all over again. Harder this time.

"Robby, wait up," a tall man with dark blond hair and a Stetson called. When he turned, Amanda saw it was Morgan Dalton, Holt's older brother—and the eldest of the five Daltons. Morgan noticed her coming his way and smiled. "Oh hey, Amanda. Nice to see you again."

At the sound of her name, Robby turned around, his mouth wide open. "Amanda!" He charged for her, wrapping his arms around her. The force of him almost knocked her over, but boy, it felt good to see him. She hugged him right back.

Amanda laughed. "Hi, Robby. And hello, Morgan. Nice to see you again too."

"Yay, Amanda's here!" Robby said.

"Robby, did you know that Daphne, who owns Happy Hearts Animal Sanctuary, officially named your very favorite cow in the pasture Daring Drake? It was as an extra thank you for adopting Bentley and Oliver and taking such great care of them."

"Really?" Robby said, beaming. "That's so awesome! If I ever meet the real Daring Drake, I'll tell him."

Daphne came out of the barn, and Morgan turned to Amanda. "Would you mind hanging with Robby for a couple minutes while I talk some business with Daphne?"

"Sure," Amanda said. *It'll break my heart to spend any time with Robby, but I sure am glad to. Wasn't that the way?* She and Daphne had had their meeting about a new outreach campaign Amanda had in mind for Happy Hearts, and Amanda had been about to leave. If the meeting had ended just a few minutes earlier, she might have missed seeing Robby at all. Fate and circumstances.

Robby walked back over to the fence and stared at Daring Drake. His whole expression had changed. From very happy to very sad. "I've been trying real hard to be better, but I guess I did something else wrong. I don't know what, though." He wiped under his eyes, and Amanda could see more tears welling.

"What do you mean, Robby?" Amanda asked, her heart going out to the boy.

"I musta done something to make you go away, Amanda," Robby said, looking up at her. "My mom left and now you left." Tears slipped down his cheeks. "Daddy said it wasn't my fault that my mom left and never visits. I believe that. But I know I musta done something to make you mad at me. I don't really even remember my mom but I remember you."

Oh, Robby, she thought, kneeling in front of him, her heart pinching in her chest. "Honey, you didn't do anything to make me mad at you. I promise, Robby. The reason I haven't been coming by is because your daddy and I had a dumb argument about me and him."

Robby brightened. "Really? Most fights *are* dumb. That's what my gram says."

"Your gram is right." Amanda gave a firm nod.

"So you don't like my dad anymore?" Robby asked. "If you two just talked and said sorry, you could be friends again like me and Ethan are."

Robby was so sweet and adorable and earnest that despite the ache in her heart, she smiled. "I do like your daddy. Very much."

"Then just tell him, Amanda. Just say sorry and he'll say sorry. And then you can come over for grilled cheese. Daddy makes the best grilled cheese." He pushed his brown bangs off his face and looked at her so expectantly.

"It's true, he does," Morgan said with a gentle smile. Amanda glanced up; she hadn't realized Holt's brother had returned. He held Amanda's gaze for a second, and by the compassion she saw in his eyes, she knew Morgan was letting her know he'd heard most of that conversation.

"And you know what, guys?" Morgan continued, "I agree that Amanda should come over and talk to your dad. Holt Dalton can be *very* stubborn."

Morgan was definitely trying to tell her something. But she'd said her piece to Holt. And he'd let her walk out of his house and life. All these days, not a word.

He was stubborn, sure. But she had her pride. Clearly Holt hadn't changed his mind or he would have come to see *her*.

"Oh yeah," Robby said, laughing. "Daddy sure is!"

Morgan grinned and ruffled his nephew's mop of hair. "Well, we'd better get going," he said, tipping his hat at Amanda.

"Bye, Amanda," Robby said, wrapping his arms around her again. "I love you."

Omigosh. He'd never said *that* before. Her heart was pure mush now. "I love you too, sweetheart." *Oh boy, do I*, she thought, watching them leave until the last bit of Robby's orange T-shirt was gone from view.

She sighed and turned to Daring Drake. "Should I go talk to Holt?" she asked the cow. "Even though the ball was left in his court?"

Daring Drake gave a little snort.

She smiled. "Was that a yes?"

I love you, Amanda... She heard Robby say it over and over in her mind. It was both very easy and very difficult to earn a child's love. It wasn't something she took lightly or for granted. She'd become special to Robby, and that meant something to him and to her.

And she loved him back. And his stubborn dad too.

Therefore, it had to be worth one more shot.

Maybe not today, though, she thought, unsure about this. She wanted Holt to come to her. He *should* come to her. That he hadn't meant he wasn't just being stubborn—he was sticking to his guns.

What to do, Daring Drake? What to do?

The day after Edward Thompson had walked off with Neal Dalton to have coffee at the main house at Dalton's Grange, ranch hand Brody Colter came grinning his way toward Holt in the big barn.

"You will never believe this," Brody said. "But Piper's dad gave us his blessing!"

Holt smiled. He wasn't the least bit surprised—now. "I'm very glad to hear that, Brody."

"He invited me over for dinner yesterday, and the four of us—me, Piper, and her parents—sat and talked. Even though we're both so young, her parents are okay that we got engaged. And like we talked about, I'm going to join the army and Piper will go to college, and once she graduates, we'll get married. Piper's mom said she was very excited to plan the wedding." Brody shook his head, a big smile on his face. "Can you believe this? I'll tell ya, man, just when you think people can't change, wham—they go ahead and change. And everyone's lives affected by them are better for it."

Holt stared at Brody, those words echoing in his head. *Just when you think people can't change...* How true was that? He thought of his father. But then he thought of himself. Holt the Unchanging.

"Mr. Thompson said he had some sense talked into him," Brody added. "If that was you, thank you. I owe you—big time."

Neal Dalton's face and trademark Stetson flashed into his mind, his father's words of wisdom turning Edward Thompson around. "Actually, you owe my dad. He did the heavy lifting."

"I'll thank him." Brody grinned. "Now I know just what people mean when say they can't wait to begin the rest of their lives. That's how I feel."

A delivery truck pulled up, and Brody put on his work gloves. Holt had to go check on Goldie, so he shook Brody's hand, wished him and Piper well and told him to call if he ever needed anything. Holt wouldn't be surprised to hear from Brody over the next bunch of years; life had a way of interfering even with the most well-thought-out plans and the fiercest of love, but he also had a very strong feeling that Brody Colter and Piper Thompson would be together forever.

As Holt entered the small barn and peered into Goldie's pen, the sweet black-and-white goat was standing up and munching on fresh hay. She was definitely out of the woods. He gave her a once-over, making a mental note to ask the vet to stop by for a final check, his thoughts drifting back to all Robby had said when the two of them had sat outside Goldilocks's pen two days straight, nursing the goat back to health.

I like to be happy.

Uncle Morgan said you can't make other people do what you want, but you can make yourself do what you want...

And then Amanda and her beautiful face came to mind.

I'd lost my ability to believe in love but my feelings for you and for Robby renewed it. I'm glad I believe—even if it means hurting this bad. Because at least I feel. *At least I* try.

That was what he needed to teach his son.

Or learn from his son. Robby was a lot wiser

than Holt in a lot of ways and seemed to know all about trying already. You *had* to try. Last night, during dinner, Robby had told Holt about him and his uncle Morgan running into Amanda at Happy Hearts.

Where it had all begun again.

He smiled as he recalled Robby's words as they'd eaten their grilled steaks and baked potatoes. *You say sorry and Amanda will say sorry and you'll be friends again.*

All around Holt, people were trying and believing, struggling and flailing, but putting themselves out there. From Amanda to Robby to Brody and Edward Thompson to Neal Dalton.

You couldn't stop trying. You couldn't give up on the most fundamental, most important thing in life: love.

Holt wasn't going to just instill that in Robby; he was going to *model* it.

He jogged the half mile back to his cabin, going to his bedroom and pulling something out from the bottom drawer of his dresser—something he'd kept hidden away for ten years.

He only hoped he wasn't too late.

When Holt arrived at Amanda's building in downtown Bronco Heights, a couple was leaving so he'd gone straight in without buzzing to let her know he was here. He didn't even know if she'd be home.

He was about to knock on her door when it opened and she took a step out, then froze, surprise lighting her beautiful face. She was dressed in exactly the outfit she'd been wearing when he ran into her at Happy Hearts. The yellow dress and short white blazer. Her dark hair was in a low ponytail.

"Holt? This is so crazy. I was just on my way to Dalton's Grange to see you."

"You were?" he asked.

She nodded. "I had something to say but since you're unexpectedly here, I'd rather you went first." She opened the door wide. "My roommate is at work, so this is good timing."

He came in, barely glancing around at the condo. He couldn't take his eyes off Amanda and wanted to tell her everything without taking a breath.

"You were wearing that outfit when we met at Happy Hearts after ten long years," he said.

She smiled and nodded. "I thought it meant the outfit is lucky."

He stared at her, hoping he understood her right. If she'd been on her way to see him and had put on her lucky outfit, the very one she wore when they ran into each other, then it wasn't too late. He could still make his comeback. *Their* comeback.

"I came over to show you something," he said. "And to ask you something." He reached into his pocket and pulled out a little pink box and opened it. "Toward the end of camp a decade ago, I bought this for you. With the money I earned that summer. I had to give half to the state to pay my fine, but the other half went toward this."

She gasped, staring at the tiny diamond, just a chip, really, on a thin gold band. She looked up at him, tears in her eyes. "I had no idea."

"I bought it back when I was still pretending to be something I wasn't. Or thought that's what I was doing. It took me until very recently to realize that *was* me that summer. The twenty-two-year-old who bought you this ring loved you, and that was all he needed to know. Then the doubts crept in and overtook him. I'm not letting that happen again."

She stared at him, waiting for him to continue.

"I'm so sorry I hurt you, Amanda. Then and now. But I love you so much. If you'll agree to give me that second chance again, I'd like to spend the rest of my life proving to you how much you mean to me, how much I want you to be my wife and Robby's mother."

Tears welled in Amanda's eyes. "You can definitely have that *second* second chance."

He put his arms around her and she wrapped hers around his neck. "Robby is going to be one happy little boy."

"We're going to be one happy little family," he said.

"Little? There's Bentley and Oliver and Poindexter, so that makes six, plus I figure we might have a kid or two in the future."

He held her tight. "I love you, Amanda Jenkins."

"I love you, Holt Dalton. And by the way, I love that ring. I love the pink box. I love that you bought it when you believed. It symbolizes a big piece of us, Holt."

She held out her left hand and he slipped the little ring with the barely visible diamond on her finger.

"One more thing," he said. "I made a stop before I got here. He reached into his other pocket and withdrew a black velvet box. When he opened it, Amanda gasped.

"Oh Holt, that is too gorgeous."

He got down on one knee, holding the box, the beautiful emerald-cut 1.5 carat diamond sparkling. "Amanda Jenkins, will you make me the happiest guy alive by marrying me and becoming my wife?"

"Yes," she whispered. "Yes!" she shouted.

He grinned and stood and slid the gold ring with the much bigger diamond right behind the little one.

She laughed and held up her hand. "Not many women can say they have two engagement rings from the same guy, bought ten years apart."

He looked at the rings on her finger, the two together symbolizing the past and present.

"Meow, me-owwww."

Holt glanced down to see Poindexter staring up at him. He picked up the big gray cat with the white paws. "Well, not many *men* can say they speak cat, but Poindexter was clearly saying he wanted to get in on the celebrating. I think you and Oliver and Bentley will make fast friends. What do you think, Poindexter?"

The cat stared at Holt with his amber eyes, but Holt didn't get another meow. He laughed and scratched the cat on his back by his tail and got a rub against his face for it. "That's a yes," he added.

"Definitely," Amanda said, her brown eyes misty. "Sorry, I'm just so overwhelmed with happiness right now I can barely form words."

"Then let's get to Dalton's Grange and tell

Robby his daddy's getting married and that he's about to get the mommy of his dreams. Robby is *never* at a loss for words." Poindexter wriggled out of his arms and jumped onto the back of the sofa, then meowed loudly as if in agreement.

"I promise you right now, Holt, I will be a great mother to Robby. I'll love him with all my heart—I do already. I'll be there for him, no matter what, in good times and bad."

"I know it," Holt said. "And thank you. For completing our lives."

"You might think this is nuts, Holt, but you know where I want to get married?"

He thought about that for a moment. "Wait. I think I do know. Is it somewhere that a cow named Daring Drake could wear a bowtie around her neck during the ceremony?"

Amanda grinned. "Exactly!"

"I think that's perfect. Happy Hearts it is."

With that settled, they headed out to Dalton's Grange to tell Robby—*their* son—that he was going to be the best man at a wedding this fall.

Happy hearts, indeed.

Epilogue

A week later, Holt was at the grill on the patio at his parents' house, keeping an eye on the burgers, chicken and ribs for many hungry Daltons, when he heard his son laughing.

He glanced over at Robby, wedged beside Amanda on one of the padded lounge chairs, a new chapter book that was two reading levels up in his hand. Bentley was on the grass beside the chair, chewing on a rawhide bone.

As Amanda ruffled Robby's hair, her engagement ring sparkled in the bright sun. They had a wedding to plan, and his son was going to be his best man, his brothers his groomsmen.

"Amanda, do you think you can find me a book about a kid who's really, really, really happy about his new mom?" Robby asked.

"I have a better idea. We can write that book together! You'll write a line, then I'll write a line. Before you know it, we'll have a whole chapter. Then another. Then another."

Robby leapt up. "Everybody, guess what? I'm getting a mom *and* I'm going to write a book!"

Neal Dalton, who was setting the huge rectangular patio table, put down the forks in his hand and walked over to his grandson for a high-five. Robby slapped him a hard one, and Neal grinned. "Are Bentley and Oliver going to be in the book?"

Robby laughed. "Yup. And you, too, Gramps. And Gram. And all my uncles. And Daring Drake. But it's mostly gonna be about how my dad and my great new mom met at Happy Hearts because I wanted a dog and Daddy said yes."

"And then Amanda said yes," Morgan quipped from his own lounge chair as he pushed his black sunglasses up on his head.

"Crazy woman," Boone added with a smirk.

Holt tossed one of Bentley's stuffed toys at Boone, which landed on his dad's shoe.

"Oh, good aim," Neal said, grinning.

Holt couldn't believe the changes in his dad in such a short time. He'd mellowed out considerably, stopping by the cabin at least once a day to see Robby, bringing a catnip toy for Oliver, throwing balls for Bentley in the yard, and letting his grandson take running leaps into his outstretched arms.

Morgan snatched the toy and chucked it, Bentley racing for it down the yard.

"Hey, Uncle Morgan," Robby said. "When are you getting married? You're older than Daddy."

That got a big laugh out of everyone.

"He's older but is he wiser?" Shep joked from his spot in a rocking chair.

Bentley brought the toy back to Morgan and dropped it at his feet. Robby ran over to his dog for a high-five, to praise how good Bentley was at playing fetch. He'd taught the dog how to high-five by giving him a ton of liver snaps for lifting up a paw to Robby's palm. The sight of that never failed to make Holt's heart skip a beat.

Morgan picked up the stuffed llama and threw it far again. "Well, Robby, if I ever meet a woman as super cool as your new mom-to-be, we'll see. But right now, the single life suits me just fine."

Holt eyed his older brother. Morgan dated—a lot. Women were always after him, handing him their cards or slips of paper with their cell phone numbers in the grocery store aisles and while in line at the coffee shop. But he never committed. Holt wondered if he ever would.

"Someday, all my sons are going to be married and giving me grandchildren," his mother said as she came out of the house with a huge bowl of homemade potato salad that she put in the center of the table.

"The more, the merrier," Neal called out, then sniffed the air. "Boy, does that smell good, Holt."

He grinned. "And everything's ready. Come and get it, folks!"

"Last one to the table is a rotten cheeseburger!" Robby shouted, taking a big head start.

"Hey, no fair," Neal said with a smile and raced him to the table.

His grandson beat him handily.

Holt laughed. He loved everyone in this yard so much. His parents, his brothers, his son, their dog.

And of course, his fiancée. He loved referring to Amanda that way but couldn't wait to replace that word with wife.

The crew headed for the table, stopping by the grill to admire Holt's skills with tongs and a spatula and knowing just when to flip. He made up two big platters of the food and set them on either end of the table.

Robby came charging at Holt and flung himself into his arms. Holt wouldn't change that about

Robby for anything. Amanda walked over, Bentley trailing, clearly hoping for his own burger.

"Can I get in on this family hug?" Amanda asked.

"Absolutely," Holt said, opening his arms wide.

Like his heart was.

* * * * *

Look for
The Maverick's Baby Arrangement
by Kathy Douglass
the next book in the new
Harlequin Special Edition continuity
Montana Mavericks:
What Happened to Beatrix?
On sale September 2020, wherever Harlequin
books and ebooks are sold.

And catch up with the previous
Montana Mavericks titles:

In Search of the Long-Lost Maverick
by New York Times *bestselling author*
Christine Rimmer

Available now!

WE HOPE YOU ENJOYED
THIS BOOK FROM

Believe in love. Overcome obstacles. Find happiness.

Relate to finding comfort and strength in the
support of loved ones and enjoy the journey
no matter what life throws your way.

6 NEW BOOKS AVAILABLE EVERY MONTH!

#2785 THE MAVERICK'S BABY ARRANGEMENT
Montana Mavericks: What Happened to Beatrix?
by Kathy Douglass

In order to retain custody of his eight-month-old niece, Daniel Dubois convinces event planner and confirmed businesswoman Brittany Brandt to marry him. It's only supposed to be a mutually beneficial business agreement...*if* they can both keep their hearts out of the equation.

#2786 THE LAST MAN SHE EXPECTED
Welcome to Starlight • by Michelle Major

When Mara Reed agrees to partner with her sworn enemy, Parker Johnson, to help a close friend, she doesn't expect the feelings of love and tenderness that complicate every interaction with the handsome attorney. Will Mara and Parker risk everything for love?

#2787 CHANGING HIS PLANS
Gallant Lake Stories • by Jo McNally

Real estate developer Brittany Doyle is eager to bring the mountain town of Gallant Lake into the twenty-first century...by changing everything. Hardware store owner Nate Thomas hates change. These opposites refuse to compromise, except when it comes to falling in love.

#2788 A WINNING SEASON
Wickham Falls Weddings • by Rochelle Alers

When Sutton Reed returns to Wickham Falls after finishing a successful baseball career, he assumes he'll just join the family business and live an uneventful life. Until his neighbor's younger brother tries to steal his car, that is. Now he's finding himself mentoring the boy—and being drawn to Zoey Allen like no one else.

#2789 IN SERVICE OF LOVE
Sutter Creek, Montana • by Laurel Greer

Commitmentphobic veterinarian Maggie is focused on training a Great Dane as a service dog and expanding the family dog-training business. Can widowed single dad Asher's belief in love after loss inspire Maggie to risk her heart and find forever with the irresistible librarian?

#2790 THE SLOW BURN
Masterson, Texas • by Caro Carson

When firefighter Caden Sterling unexpectedly delivers Tana McKenna's baby by the side of the road, the unlikely threesome forms a special bond. Their flirty friendship slowly becomes more, until Tana's ex and the truth about her baby catches up with her. Can she win back the only man who can make this family complete?

Real estate developer Brittany Doyle is eager to bring the mountain town of Gallant Lake into the twenty-first century...by changing everything. Hardware store owner Nate Thomas hates change. These opposites refuse to compromise, except when it comes to falling in love.

Read on for a sneak peek at
Changing His Plans,
the next book in the Gallant Lake Stories miniseries by Jo McNally.

He stuck his head around the corner of the fasteners aisle just in time to see a tall brunette stagger into the revolving seed display. Some of the packets went flying, but she managed to steady the display before the whole thing toppled. He took in what probably had been a very nice silk blouse and tailored trouser suit before she was drenched in the storm raging outside. The heel on one of the ridiculously high heels she was wearing had snapped off, explaining why she was stumbling around.

"Having a bad morning?"

The woman looked up in annoyance, strands of dark, wet hair falling across her face.

"You could say that. I don't suppose you have a shoe repair place in this town?" She looked at the bright red heel in her hand.

Nate shook his head as he approached her. "Nope. But hand it over. I'll see what I can do."

A perfectly shaped brow arched high. "Why? Are you going to cobble them back together with—" she gestured around widely "—maybe some staples or screws?"

"Technically, what you just described is the definition of cobbling, so yeah. I've got some glue that'll do the trick." He met her gaze calmly. "It'd be a lot easier to do if you'd take the shoe off. Unless you also think I'm a blacksmith?"

He was teasing her. Something about this soaking-wet woman still having so much…regal bearing…amused Nate. He wasn't usually a fan of the pearl-clutching country club set who strutted through Gallant Lake on the weekends and referred to his family's hardware store as "adorable." But he couldn't help admiring this woman's ability to hold on to her superiority while looking like she accidentally went to a water park instead of the business meeting she was dressed for. To be honest, he also admired the figure that expensive red suit was clinging to as it dripped water on his floor.

He held out his hand. "I'm Nate Thomas. This is my store."

She let out an irritated sigh. "Brittany Doyle." She slid her long, slender hand into his and gripped with surprising strength. He held it for just a half second longer than necessary before shaking off the odd current of interest she invoked in him.

Don't miss
Changing His Plans *by Jo McNally,*
available September 2020 wherever
Harlequin Special Edition books and ebooks are sold.

Harlequin.com